# THE CLOVERLEAF
# CATTLE COMPANY

Bessie Thomas believed in miracles, and her husband, Jawn Henry, did not. But after finding a murdered settler and his woman, and running down the renegades responsible — taking care of them the way justice dictated, but the law did not — Jawn Henry would have time to reflect. He and Bessie had never had children. Miracles evidently did happen.

*Books by Lauran Paine*
*in the Linford Western Library:*

**TRAIL TO TROUBLE**

LAURAN PAINE

# THE CLOVERLEAF CATTLE COMPANY

*Complete and Unabridged*

# LINFORD
*Leicester*

First published in Great Britain in 1992 by
Robert Hale Limited
London

First Linford Edition
published 1997
by arrangement with
Robert Hale Limited
London

British Library CIP Data

Paine, Lauran, 1916–
The Cloverleaf Cattle Company.—Large print ed.—
Linford western library
1. American fiction—20th century
2. Large type books
I. Title
813.5'4 [F]

ISBN 0-7089-5050-7

Published by
F. A. Thorpe (Publishing) Ltd.
Anstey, Leicestershire
Set by Words & Graphics Ltd.
Anstey, Leicestershire
Printed and bound in Great Britain by
T. J. Press (Padstow) Ltd., Padstow, Cornwall

This book is printed on acid-free paper

# 1

## Beginning

TWENTY years had passed since Jawn Henry Thomas used three silver dollars, two side by side, one above, to show the blacksmith the design of the branding iron he wanted him to make.

The blacksmith, an elderly, taciturn individual who was rarely without a cud in his cheek, had studied the dollars for a moment, than had said, "You goin' to call it the three dollar brand?"

Jawn Henry looked exasperated. "A Cloverleaf. That's what a cloverleaf looks like."

The blacksmith continued to study the three cartwheels on the earthen floor of his smithy. He shrugged. It seemed to him that cloverleaves only had two petals, but he was unsure about that and it made no difference anyway. Jawn Henry wanted what seemed to the blacksmith to be three balls, two on the bottom and one on top. The blacksmith would make it for him. But he had a question: "Two cow irons, or one cow iron and a horse iron?"

"One cow iron," Jawn Henry replied. He'd only recently brought his cows to three hundred; he was clearing a profit about like wages, but knew for a blessed fact that this time next year, or the year after, he wouldn't have to watch his pennies.

The blacksmith asked if Jawn Henry was in a hurry, because the blacksmith had four wheels to sweat tyres onto, a buggy axle to re-build and install, and some horses out back to be shod.

Jawn Henry's home place was six miles west of town. It was late spring, a mite late for calving but some of his cows were still dropping them and the ones already on the ground were a tad young for marking and branding. He said, "Two weeks?" and the blacksmith smiled. They shook hands, Jawn Henry went up to the general store, left his list with the clerk, pointed past the window where a battered light wagon was parked, a hefty horse drowsing between the shafts, hiked over to the Templeton Cafe and ate enough for two men. The cafeman watched and wondered how anyone could eat like a horse and not be fat enough to butcher.

Jawn Henry was thirty-five, a tad under six feet and weighed about a hundred and sixty pounds, bone, muscle and sinew. Probably the main reason he did not weigh more was because a three hundred head cattle outfit was what one man could care for, by working from sunup until sundown. Until a rancher had at least four-five hundred head he did not clear enough profit to hire someone.

Jawn Henry figured that would be next year, too. Unless something came up, then he'd have to wait another year.

Outside, the town was lively, buggies passed, horsemen split off until the rigs passed then came together again. Some tow-headed kids followed by a grinning brindle dog whose mother probably had no idea who the brindle dog's pappy was, were walking southward, heads down as they scuffed dust at the edge of the plankwalk; sometimes they got lucky and found a dime or a penny.

A fairly new stage coach entered town at a dead walk. Both doors had the same legend: Templeton Stage & Cartage Company. Templeton Arizona Territory.

Jawn Henry crossed over and hiked in the direction of the livery barn, which was in the middle of town with the jailhouse to the north and the Templeton Grand Hotel to the south.

He had been in the country long enough to know most of the merchants. His favourite was a bandy-legged gnome of a grizzled man named Tom Clancy. The moment Jawn Henry appeared in the runway the older man appeared. He had been mending harness and had the dry bees wax on his hands to prove it. He said, "Did you get it across to him?"

"Yeah, I drew a diagram in the dust of his floor."

Clancy looked unconvinced. "He's a good smith, son, but kind of thick upstairs. You want your horse?"

Jawn Henry nodded, watched the bow-legged gnome go out back and return leading Jawn Henry's slightly pigeon-toed bay with the slightly slanty eyes.

As he was saddling Clancy said, "You need a man yet?"

"Maybe next year. Can't afford one right now."

Clancy sat on a wall bench as he said, "There's a feller about your age sleepin' in my wagon shed. He needs work. I lent him a couple dollars to eat on."

Jawn Henry turned the horse to lead him outside before mounting him. Only gunsels and greenhorns mounted horses inside buildings. "I could use a man, Tom," he told the liveryman, "but I'm not big enough yet to stand the expense. Maybe next year."

Clancy knew about ranching, which is why he had quit long ago, moved to town and bought the livery barn. "I've seen your place. Looked to me like you got maybe four, five hundred head."

Jawn Henry shook his head. "Close to three hundred mammy cows, an' eight bulls."

Tom Clancy was one of those people you could tie to the tail of a wild horse and he still would not give up. He nodded at the bay horse, bridled, saddled, and standing patiently. "You goin' to tie him to the tailgate of your wagon?"

Jawn Henry nodded.

Old Clancy stood up. "How long you had that horse?"

"Two months; bought him from In'ians who was trailing through."

"You pay over ten dollars for him?"

"Twenty dollars. Why, you want to buy him?"

"No. Do you hobble or tie him?"

"Hobble him. Clancy what — ?"

"Jawn Henry I tied that son of a bitch out back yestiddy an' he set back, busted the shank, tore the cross-member of my tie-rack, an' if you tie him to the tailgate of your wagon he'll bust it sure as hell, an' maybe do worse."

The younger man turned to look at his bay horse. He hadn't had occasion to tie him solid since he'd owned him. When he'd ridden him, he'd used hobbles because in his part of the Territory, while there was brush and grass and rocks, there were precious few trees. Mostly, rangemen in this country hobbled their animals.

Tom Clancy brightened. "I got the solution. Unless you want to let him stay here at two-bits a day until you can go to town again. This feller I was tellin' you about who lives in my shed. He's a rangeman if I ever saw one. My guess is that if you — "

"I told you, Tom. It'll be a while before I'm set up to where I can hire a rider."

"Feed him, let him bed down in your barn. He'll work for his keep."

Jawn Henry was becoming annoyed. "How do you know what he'll work for?"

"Jawn Henry, he's been in my shed for goin' onto two weeks. I an' him got pretty well acquainted. I know for a fact he'll do it. Now then, you want your wagon busted to hell by that halter-pulling bay horse, or you want to kill two birds with one stone; let him ride your horse back, and give him his keep for work."

Jawn Henry stood beside the bay horse eyeing Tom Clancy. It had been the liveryman's drawing in the dust that had inspired Jawn Henry Thomas to adopt that cloverleaf sign for his branding iron. "Where is he?" he asked.

Tom Clancy jutted his jaw. "Over at

8

the emporium. He's to fetch me back some liniment and wrapping cloth. I got to fire a horse I traded for that's got a bowed tendon. He'll be along, just set and I'll tell you what I know about him. His name's Bradford Holifield. He's about your size and build. Sort of quiet."

"How come he hasn't got a job? Hell Tom, the big outfits are hiring this time of year."

"Got no way to ride out."

"You could loan him a horse."

"I put nine head out to pasture a few days before he showed up. I dassn't let any go that I got left. Even now I'm short a few I could have hired out lately."

Before Jawn Henry could speak again a tallish, lean man came in from the roadway. The men on the bench could see him better than he could see them. He'd been in bright sunlight, their eyes had adjusted to the interior gloom.

Clancy arose to accept the sack the stranger had, and jerked his head in

Jawn Henry's direction. "Brad, this here is Jawn Henry Thomas. He's got a small outfit west of town . . . You want to hire out for your keep?"

Holified regarded Jawn Henry through a moment of silence, then nodded his head without speaking.

Clancy beamed. "There you are, Jawn Henry, an' you don't have to wait no year or two."

There was something about Bradford Holifield's reserve that made Jawn Henry slow to shake the other man's hand, which signified acceptance of the man, on those terms. For almost a hundred years west of the Missouri river, a handclasp had been the way men made agreements. The reason was simple, west of the Missouri illiteracy was higher than anywhere else in the nation.

Jawn Henry had a couple of questions. "You worked cattle much?" he asked.

Holified, who had sunk-set dark eyes and a wide mouth, nodded. "Most of my life, Mister Thomas. New Messico, a short spell in west Texas, up north. Whatever I got to do, I expect I've done it a dozen times before."

Tom Clancy, watching them both, thought Jawn Henry was having doubts. But they had shaken hands so he said, "You're not gettin' married. If it don't work . . . " Clancy shrugged.

Jawn Henry handed the reins of his bay horse to Holifield, led the way across the road to the emporium, where his wagon had been loaded, and as he climbed to the box, unlooped the lines and set his booted foot to release the binders, he said, "Anythin' you got to do before we leave town?"

Holifield shook his head.

They left town heading west under a day which might have been summer-warm except for a chilly wind coming out of the north.

All that had happened close to twenty years earlier. Brad Holifield and Jawn Henry never had an argument, even when Holifield was told to do something he disagreed with.

11

Jawn Henry's range expanded, his herd was almost a thousand mammy-cows and bulls on a ratio of one to forty.

Riders had come and gone, Jawn Henry married a woman named Bessie White. Her father who died six years after the marriage, had owned the emporium in Templeton.

Jawn Henry finally yielded and had a new saddle made although for the life of him he could not understand why it was necessary. With minimum care, which is a little less care than most saddles got, a man's saddle out-lasted its owner.

He acquired several buildings in Templeton, which his wife oversaw. He had made it clear that he did not like riding to town to collect rents.

Brad Holifield had been rangeboss of the Cloverleaf Cattle Company for six years. He got foreman's pay and lived comfortably in the leanto built off the back of the bunkhouse. He still did a day's work with the seasonal riders, and when Cloverleaf got large enough to require three men year round, Brad Holifield counted as one of them.

Over the years that he and Jawn Henry had built up the herd and land holdings, he had not changed from that day years back when he had been hired for his keep. He spoke when the need arose, otherwise he said nothing.

Bessie was curious. Jawn Henry had yielded to his wife's town ways of owning buildings, and was generally tolerant, but Jawn Henry put his foot down about the rangeboss.

They had been married almost three years before she started asking questions. What he told her then he would have told her when they were grey if she asked, but Bessie Thomas was a wise woman. She only brought up the topic one more time, and that was after a runaway damned green colt had killed itself going over a bluff and came within an ace of killing its rider.

Jawn Henry was bed-fast for two months. According to the doctor from

Templeton — the town had also grown during those years — Jawn Henry should not even attempt to stand, let alone walk, for six months. His back hadn't been broken but there were cracked vertebrae. The doctor, an unsmiling stork of a man, had told Bessie if her husband did not do as the doctor said, he would not be responsible.

It was a warm summer evening three hours before the sun went down that the rangeboss came to sit beside the bed and discuss the matter of encroaching home-steaders. Bessie heard them from the kitchen, but only their voices, the words were indistinguishable.

After Brad had departed she took a cup of hot herb tea to her husband. He had been a lifelong drinker of black coffee. He drank her concoctions because he knew she meant well, but every blessed cupful she brought him tasted like boiled bugs.

It was too hot. He sipped then set the cup aside. Bessie, a handsome woman, one of those female-women who hadn't been pretty as a girl, but who became pretty in their full maturity, asked if Jawn Henry would like her to read to him.

He shook his head. Settlers had been arriving over the last few years. He'd heard tales of their encroachment from other stockmen. It worried him less than it irritated him.

His wife asked a question. "Jawn Henry — suppose your back don't ever get like it was before? The doctor wouldn't say whether you could ride a horse again or not."

Jawn Henry's normal disposition was even, rather tolerant, un-demanding. Men who rode for him liked him without exception. He and Brad Holifield had over the years had some laughs together.

As a bed-patient he reacted to his situation the way most active outdoorsmen reacted. He was restless and irritable. "That consarned bean pole. Every time he walks in here he not only dresses like an undertaker, I get a suspicion he is surprised that I'm still here . . . I'll ride again, Bess. You can bet on it!"

Bessie smoothed her skirt, studied her hands for a moment before speaking again. "I was thinking of Brad . . ."

"What about Brad!"

Bessie waited before speaking again. She had come to understand her husband's peevishness, to understand the reason for it and to sympathise.

"You'll ride again, dear," she told him, saw the fire dwindle in his gaze and let another moment pass before she also said, "Daddy taught me to hope for the best and to expect the worst."

Jawn Henry's expression was wooden. He and her father had gotten along because they worked at it, but since they had nothing in common, they had remained acquaintances without being friends. To Jawn Henry it had been a case of treating the cow well in order to get the calf.

"Suppose something happened to either one of us, Jawn Henry. Maybe to one of us but not the other."

He turned his head toward her on the pillow. "The other one would make out, Bess. We got money, cattle, the ranch, the buildings in town."

"Suppose it happened to you — "

"It won't, but if it did you could depend on Brad."

Bessie fumbled in a pocket beneath her apron, unfolded a dog-eared large piece of paper and held it where her husband could see it.

He read, glanced away then re-read it. "Where did you get that thing?" he exclaimed.

"From Daddy."

He was big-eyed. "He knew? You mean to tell me your paw knew for years an' never said anything?"

"You were my husband. I loved you. That was important to him, Jawn Henry."

"Did he say where he got that wanted dodger?"

17

"No dear, he never did. He gave it to me a few days before he died . . . Jawn Henry . . . ?"

He snarled. "I don't believe he murdered anyone but even if he did, that wanted poster is almost twenty years old."

# 2

## A Degree of Recovery

IT was four weeks before the medicine man agreed that Jawn Henry could sit out front on the porch. But he was to walk no farther than the porch, and under no circumstances was to go off the porch.

A month made a difference. Jawn Henry's legs were unreliable, Bessie helped, clinging to him and that was irritating too.

His all-weather tan had faded to white. He sat in a chair out front, watched Brad and the other two Cloverleaf riders head out, swore fiercely to himself about his fate, and ate more than he had up to this time which was gratifying to his wife, who had been diplomatically urging him to eat more in order so that he would regain his lost weight.

For a solid week he occupied the chair under the porch overhang, shielded from the summer which had arrived since his injury. He watched the riders leave and sometimes he was still out there when they returned.

Brad visited him when he could. They discussed the weather, which had been favourable lately so grass was strong, the cattle, an encroachment on their easterly range where a settler had taken up land, built a sod house and planted a potato crop which Cloverleaf cattle had found irresistible, so the squatter had set up a straw-stuffed dummy. The cows were reticent for a few days, then got bold and ignored the dummy. Brad said he and his companions had heard some shooting so they rode over there. The settler had run the cattle off by firing a shotgun over their heads. Brad said when he saw the Cloverleaf riders, he warned them that unless they kept their damned cattle out of the potato patch he was going to lower the shotgun and they could drag away the carcasses.

Brad said the squatter had a wife, a drab woman, and two kids, a boy and a girl about ten and twelve years old.

Jawn Henry sat in silence for a while. Folks had been saying settlers were inevitable since the government had established homesteading rights and the railroad, which had been given every other section of land as an inducement, had been selling off plots a hundred and sixty acres each to encourage folks to come west.

He and his wife's father had once had a conversation about settlers. Bessie's paw favoured them, they would increase business at his store. Jawn Henry had not favoured them. Her father had told Jawn Henry the only legal way he could protect his range was to get title to it.

At first Jawn Henry had balked, but after a while he had set aside so much money each autumn, and had bought land.

21

He had done this the shrewd way. Settlers were no different from cattle; they had to have water. Jawn Henry had bought land where creeks ran, where springs existed, and where catch-basins came naturally with the lie of the land.

He owned sources of water, so, he thought, he did not have to go on buying land where there was no water. He had, nevertheless, bought up hundreds of acres of the best grassland just to be on the safe side. He could afford it.

Over where the settler had put down roots, Jawn Henry owned the range very close to the homesteader. Since most of his land had not been surveyed, he wasn't sure he did not own the land where the settler had squatted.

Brad doubted that. His reason was elemental. The railroad had surveying crews in the country for several years. He told Jawn Henry the railroad had to do that in order to give legal title to settlers.

Brad suggested the cattle be kept off that part of the range. Jawn Henry had replied irritably to that. "For how long? Forever? Then we'd need another rider or two just to patrol over there. Besides, that's part of our summer graze. If we put cattle on the winter ground in summer, there wouldn't be enough grass to see them through . . . No, we got to figure out something about that squatter. What's his name?"

"Carl Mackensen. Sort of husky built feller a little younger'n you an me."

"Potatoes," exclaimed Jawn Henry. "The damned fool, don't he know it don't rain enough in this country to bring up a crop of potatoes?"

"He's digging a well."

Jawn Henry looked at his rangeboss. "Did he tell you that?"

"No, we saw where he's digging."

"Did you tell him he'll have to dig to China? There's no water. Other folks have dug wells. Unless it's on the surface or comes from above . . . Did you tell him, Brad?"

"No. We didn't talk much. He was mad and had a shotgun. We gathered the cattle and drove them a couple miles northeasterly."

After the rangeboss departed Bessie came out to herd Jawn Henry inside for supper. He told her what Brad had said. She did not comment until they were half through supper, then reminded him what her father had warned would happen and how inevitable her father had felt settling up the country would be.

That kind of talk did not help either Jawn Henry's disposition or his digestion. After supper he went to bed down, found a cigar he had forgotten he had, and lay awake until Bessie came along, attracted by something she thought was burning rope, took the cigar, which was down to a stub anyway, opened the bedroom window and sat on the bedside chair. She knew her husband's moods. He really only had two: Good natured and bad natured. She told him not to mind the settler, she — and Jawn Henry — had seen them settle in before, and in a year or two they were gone.

His reply to that was: "But they never faced Cloverleaf with a shotgun, Bessie."

She studied his brooding expression, decided — mistakenly — it was another example of the peevishness which was the result of his incapacity, and changed the subject.

"Dobie came by a while back on his way home. He asked how you were, when I told him, he laughed and said some cracked bones wouldn't hold down a good man, you'd be on your feet directly."

Jawn Henry's gaze drifted enquiringly toward his wife. "Kind of late, wasn't it?"

"Yes. He'd been to Templeton . . . I met him on the porch — he'd been drinking."

Jawn Henry pondered that. Folks called him Doughbelly, or just plain Dobie, but his real name was Dudley

Pierce. He ranched northwesterly of Cloverleaf, had a respectable outfit, two riders, ran cattle along the foothills, had never married and attributed that condition to living his life the way the good Lord intended a man to do. Have a drink now and then, smoke up the house if he wanted to, eat with hired hands at the bunkhouse, and bathe only when the river was shallow and the water warm.

Dobie was shrewd. He'd come into the country a few years later than Jawn Henry had, and while they had been good neighbours since, neither had been the visiting or hob-nobbing sort, so they had gotten along better than most outfits who had several miles of adjoining range.

Bessie was not fond of Doughbelly Pierce, for her own reasons which she had only rarely allowed to surface because she knew her husband and their raffish neighbour were friends.

Jawn Henry asked if Dobie had brought any news from town. He had, she said, and sat primly looking at the hands in her lap as she told her husband what Doughbelly had told her — and had laughed about.

"A settler braced the marshal in Templeton . . . The same man Brad met a few days back."

"And — well, what did Dobie say about that?"

"The settler knocked Mister Hogston down, took away his revolver, unloaded it in the centre of Main Street with half the town looking on, flung the gun away and rode his work horse out of town."

Jawn Henry's eyes popped wide, for a moment he was speechless, then he laughed as Dobie had done while his wife got red in the face. Her father had indoctrinated her from an early age to respect the law, its enforcers, the church and its pastors, and his store along with the man who had founded and who owned it.

Jawn Henry had known the town marshal for several years. He had come from somewhere down in Texas to replace the older former town marshal who had retired and moved away.

Arnie Hogston was big, a tad better than six feet and weighed better than two hundred pounds. His only failing in the eyes of folks like Jawn Henry was his youth — he claimed to be a little past thirty. He was actually twenty-five, had lied because towns normally preferred older, more seasoned law enforcers.

But Marshal Hogston's real problem was that he did not look even twenty-five. He had the complexion and general appearance of an eighteen-year-old. But the town council had hired him anyway. As the chairman had said, they'd only received two applications, one from a notorious drunk named Shag Callahan, and Arnie Hogston. There really had been no alternative.

Up until now Arnie had handled things well, kept order, enforced town ordinances, was well-liked and it was said, was both fast and accurate with his handgun — one of those remarks which circulated because men who wore guns for a living were just naturally assumed to be good with them, but in Arnie Hogston's place, no one had ever actually seen him use his Colt. He'd only been local law enforcer for a little more than a year.

Jawn Henry stopped laughing. Brad's earlier description of that settler facing his riders with a shotgun, came to mind more solidly than before. Brad hadn't seemed impressed. But . . . After Bessie left Jawn Henry lay in dusk-light wondering if perhaps he did not have a new neighbour it would do well not to think of too contemptuously.

The following morning he took a cup of coffee to the front porch with him, sat down and contemplated dying tendrils of smoke rising over the bunkhouse, his empty yard and depleted horse-corral. Heat would be along directly. Spring never lasted long. If Jawn Henry'd had his way the seasons would be reversed, summer would come early and hot, last only maybe a month, then cool, pleasant springtime would arrive and last until autumn.

He drained the cup, left it on the porch floor beside his chair, heard his wife leave by the kitchen door for the routine watering and weeding of her garden patch before it became hot, arose, navigated the three wide steps with care and the support of a railing, halted on level ground, hitched at his britches and began walking. He reached the barn, entered, made for an old chair with a hair-side-up rawhide seat and eased down.

His legs were a little achy, he had not walked that far since last autumn, otherwise he felt well enough. His back was neither tight nor sore.

The sum total of his experience was suppressed jubilation. He sat for about ten minutes, than arose and returned to the porch, was sitting there beside his empty coffee cup when Bessie came out with a sweat-shiny face full of high colour from exertion, and handed Jawn

Henry a tall glass of cold water.

She sat down nearby in her rocker, sipped cold water, dabbed at sweat, and smiled because her pole beans, peas, acorn squash and corn were sprouting. It had been years since the Thomas's had needed to supplement their meat diet with a garden of vegetables, but Bessie still planted, cultivated and harvested as she had done the first five or six years after they were married.

Other ranch folk did the same, except the others usually had anywhere from two to ten younguns to do the weeding and picking. Bessie and Jawn Henry had never had children and never talked about it, but if effort would have counted for anything, in their earlier years they would have filled a barn with children.

It simply had never happened. Privately each had their own explanation. For Bess it had been the will of God. For Jawn Henry it was the result of too many bucking horses.

As they sat with their cold water, with heat increasing, but protected by the overhang of their front porch which ran the full length of the front of the house, neither was disposed to conversation until each had rested from their labour. Then Bessie said, "You look much better, Jawn Henry. This is the first time I've seen good colour in your face in a while."

He would not have told her what he had done if she'd held a gun to his head. He smiled over at her. "Your cookin', Bess. You're world's better for me than that damned stork that dresses like an undertaker."

She remonstrated. "Doctor Farrar is responsible for you being able to sit in that chair. He's a good physician and you know it."

Jawn Henry's interest wandered. It was time to move cattle to the higher part of the range where they would remain until autumn, when they would be drifted to winter feed.

The hard work had been completed

a month or so ago; marking, branding, culling and doctoring, the only really hard, and at times dangerous, work of range stockmen.

They would make a gather at the end of summer for animals to be trailed down to the railroad corrals, sixty miles southeast of Templeton.

Henry watched a thin distant banner of dust; this autumn he would ride with the others.

Bessie suddenly scattered his thoughts. "When I was in the garden this morning I saw two children . . . They were hiding in some bushes watching me. A young girl and a boy."

Jawn Henry turned slowly. "That damned settler's kids?"

"Possibly. They'd have been a long way from home though. But there aren't any other youngsters around that I know of."

Jawn Henry's frown lingered. The settler's place had to be a good three miles northeast. "Did they have horses, Bess?"

"I didn't see horses. There could have been, but it seemed more likely they were afoot."

Jawn Henry nodded. "Well, when you're that young three, four miles don't seem far." He sat in silence for a moment before speaking again. "I'll have Brad put a stop to them sneakin' around spyin' on folks."

Bessie arose to take their empty glasses inside. She said nothing more about the children; privately, she regretted mentioning them. Her husband's final remark and his dark look told her clearly that he had been irritated.

That evening Brad came to the main house to tell Jawn Henry they had moved the cattle, and had found eight or ten head of Dobie's critters mixed in.

This had happened before, even as Dobie Pierce had found Cloverleaf cattle with his stock. Since there were no fences it was customary to make the cut and drift the trespassing cattle back to their home range.

Except that this time Brad had something else to report. "There was barefoot horse tracks where two riders had choused them cattle."

Jawn Henry regarded his rangeboss quizzically. "That don't make much sense, does it?"

Brad's reply was quietly given. "Not ordinarily, but that settler's kids was riding a pair of big pudding-footed harness horses."

"You saw them?"

"Yes. Back a few mornings. They was coming south behind some cattle. They saw us and ran like scairt rabbits."

Jawn Henry sighed. That gawddamned squatter was beginning to annoy the hell out of him. "Tell you what. If you'll hitch the driving buggy in the morning, I'll drive over there."

Brad gazed at Jawn Henry in silence for a long moment, then nodded and departed. Fifteen minutes later Bessie arrived in the bedroom with a bowl of stew and a cup of hot broth. She said nothing until her husband was eating, then she spoke firmly.

"You're not going to drive the buggy over to the settler's place, Jawn Henry."

His eyes rose to her face. She knew that look even before he replied. "Bess, I been a model of patience. I've done everything that damned stork'n you have told me to do. It's been six months since I got hurt."

"That's uneven country, Jawn Henry." Bess thought a compromise might work so she said, "Take Brad with you. Let him drive. I'll fit some cushions for you to set on."

"Bess, Brad's got work to do. He can't just — "

"Then I'll drive you over there."

Jawn Henry reddened. He intended to put the fear of God and Mister Winchester into the heart of that settler, which would be impossible if the squatter saw him being driven over there by a woman.

He did not argue. He said, "All right. Tell Brad him an' I'll go over there first thing in the morning."

Bessie waited until the bowl and cup were empty, took them back to the kitchen, shed her apron and hiked down to the bunkhouse.

# 3

## The Settler

TO people who lived according to omens, a beautiful sunbright morning with promise of pleasant warmth later was a good omen. What saved that kind of omen from a foreboding of drought was a wide band of dirty clouds stretched around the distant bow-shaped mountains. It was going to rain; maybe not today or tomorrow, those black clouds were barely moving, but rain would come.

Speculating about when the storm would arrive occupied Brad and his employer for part of the drive to the Mackensen place. Afterwards, watching the rude part dugout house of the settler as they approached it, their conversation turned to the man who lived up ahead.

Brad hadn't heard about the settler's run-in with Marshal Hogston. After Jawn Henry had related the incident as his wife had gotten it from Dobie Pierce, Brad was quiet right up until they saw two children dash for the house like their lives depended upon reaching it before the oncoming buggy got close . . . Then all he said was, "This'll be like hittin' a beehive with a stick."

He was correct. As they came even with some stirred ground where tiny sprouts showed, a stocky man emerged from the house. As far as Jawn Henry could see, the man was unarmed. So was Jawn Henry, but his rangeboss's holstered Colt was visible.

Brad was careful to drive completely around the potato patch and draw the lines only when about fifty feet separated the rig from the rugged-looking, sandy-haired man who was waiting.

Jawn Henry said, "Good morning."

The brawny man nodded. "Same to you."

Jawn Henry leaned forward under the buggy top. "I'm Jawn Henry Thomas of Cloverleaf."

The sandy-headed man with a lipless wide mouth and deep-set grey eyes acknowledged that with a nod. "I'm Carl Mackensen. I talked with that gent with you, but don't know his name."

"Brad Holifield, my rangeboss."

Again the burly man nodded but this time said nothing. Brad also nodded and also remained silent.

"Mister Mackensen, my range boundary is pretty close to your potato patch."

"I know that, Mister Thomas. There's a piece of pipe drove in the ground where my homestead borders Cloverleaf." Mackensen pointed. "There was some rocks piled atop it, but my kids used them to pelt birds out of the potato patch."

Jawn Henry was not very interested in the survey marker. "You got a pair of harness horses, Mister Mackensen?"

"Yes sir. I got four horses, three for

harness and one for ridin'. The ridin' horse is a combination animal."

Jawn Henry asked Brad the colour of the horses he and his companions had seen driving cattle. Brad's answer was brusque. "Big sorrel an' a big bay."

Jawn Henry asked if Mackensen's work-stock were those colours. The man on the ground nodded. "That'll be mine, most likely. You saw 'em somewhere?"

"No, but a few days back my riders saw them driving a little bunch of cattle. They run off. Mister Mackensen, those cattle belong to a rancher named Pierce some miles northeast. I got no idea where your children was when they picked up the cattle, but I do know they drove Mister Pierce's cattle down among my cattle."

"You know for a fact it was my children, Mister Thomas?"

Brad answered. "A girl with pigtails, maybe ten or twelve, and a tow-headed lad about the same age or thereabouts.

41

The girl was riding the sorrel work horse, the lad was atop the bay. Bareback. When they saw us coming they ran over this way."

"You didn't follow them, Mister Holifield?"

"No. We wanted to keep those Pierce cattle clear of ours. We headed them back the way they had been driven. In a day or such a matter we'll take time off to drive them back to Mister Pierce's range."

Mackensen glanced in the direction of his house. There was no sign of anyone over there. He sighed and loosened a little as he said, "Mister Thomas, them children is at the age where they're more trouble than a bag full of ants. I let them take the horses now an' again. I'll tan their hides an' maybe work it out some way for the trouble you been put to. I'm short on cash money, but I'll — "

"One thing, Mister Mackensen," Jawn Henry said. "Do you know

42

where those children were yesterday morning?"

"Well . . . Somewhere around."

"They was hid in some brush a short ways from where my wife's got a garden patch, spyin' on her."

Mackensen began to colour. "That's quite a hike, isn't it, Mister Thomas? There could be other kids — "

"There are no other young children closer than town," Jawn Henry said. "It'd be about three miles over an' three miles back. What time did your children show up in the afternoon?"

Mackensen answered shortly. "I first seen them just short of suppertime. I been busy layin' out where I figure to put a barn."

Jawn Henry's gaze left the settler long enough to consider the yard, a brush enclosure where chickens were making noise, and mounds of dirt where a well was being dug.

Mackensen interrupted Jawn Henry's thoughts. "I'll ask the children, Mister Thomas. If it was them over spyin' on your yard I'll fix 'em so's they'll eat standin' up for a week."

Jawn Henry's gaze at the thin-lipped, steady-eyed brawny man made him regret mentioning the spying incident as much as Bessie had regretted mentioning it to him. He cleared his throat. "When I was a youngster I done things like that. You most likely did too, Mister Mackensen."

The settler did not yield an inch. "What we done we got shellacked for. That's how we learned . . . If there's nothin' more . . . " Mackensen bobbed his head and strode purposefully toward the house.

Brad talked up the horse, made a big sashay and was heading west when he and Jawn Henry heard a child scream. Brad drove wooden-faced. Jawn Henry loosened his collar. It was warm. They heard another scream shortly before they were beyond earshot, and that time Brad Holifield spoke.

"When I was a youngster I turned some mules out where there was cattle.

The feller I worked for — room and board — lit into me with a quirt."

They drove a mile before either of them spoke again. Jawn Henry could see his rooftop. "No point in tellin' Miz Thomas what we heard."

Brad drove in hard silence all the way into the yard, avoided looking at Jawn Henry even when the other man was walking across toward the yard. Brad was busy parking the buggy in its three-sided shed, caring for the harness animal, and afterwards tucking a cud into his cheek out back near a round corral which had a large stone trough in it near where a shaggy mulberry tree had birds by the dozen this time of year.

There were times when a man could go for years without remembering, then, something like those screaming youngsters, plunged him back in time to his own difficulties as a youth.

But Holifield was old enough now to have, for the most part, refused to allow himself to dwell on subjects that, if dwelt upon often had a tendency to corrode the soul and embitter the mind.

He had settled the score with that Dutchman who had beat him regularly with a leather tug. It had taken a few years, but now the score was settled, the past was done.

One of the other riders came out back, saw Brad and said, "You'n Jawn Henry go over an' talk to that darned settler?"

Brad said they had, and that the settler had been more civil than Brad had expected him to be. The cowboy, a wiry, lean man named Sam Nesbitt, who had perpetually squinted grey eyes, was nodding his head as he went closer to see if the trough needed the plug pulled to let in more water. "I was up north when them Wyoming livestock growers went to war with sheepmen."

Brad remembered that lurid and bloody affair. He asked if Nesbitt had been involved. The cowboy was leaning to pull the plug, which dripped, when he replied. "Well, yes I rode for one of the fellers who was in the association, but me'n some others was never sent where the brawling took place . . . What I started out to say was that I knew some of them settlers. Ate at their shacks a time or two when I was caught too far out. Couple of 'em I'd meet in town an' we'd swap drinks . . . The sheep part of it didn't set no better with me than it set with any other cowman, but if they'd asked me to shoot them fellers I wouldn't have done it . . . Maybe this squatter's got a right to try'n scratch out a living."

Brad watched Sam Nesbitt pound the plug back in the pipe with his fist. When Nesbitt started back up through the barn they exchanged nods.

Brad jettisoned his cud, rinsed his mouth at the trough and turned to also go up through to the yard.

It wasn't the settler. Not exactly anyway. It was the kids. Well, maybe it *was* Mackensen because he sure larruped the hell out of them. Still

47

and all, like he had said, and like everyone knew, horses, dogs and kids only understood a larrupin now and then to know what they could do and what they couldn't do.

Brad headed for the bunkhouse where someone had already started the stove to smoking. Over at the main house the stovepipe shimmered with very little smoke; the fire over there had been burning longer.

Jawn Henry did a fair job of censoring what he told his wife. She, on the other hand, was much less interested in the squatter than in Jawn Henry's welfare. She wanted to know if his back ached. He shook his head, went to the cupboard for some whiskey to tip into the coffee, and sat back down.

"How about your hips?" his wife asked. "Your legs?"

Jawn Henry sipped laced coffee and regarded Bessie fondly. It had taken time to become accustomed to having someone worry, get real solicitous and all. Jawn Henry had never had that before. He appreciated it and dearly cared for his wife, but sometimes her anxiety over his welfare felt sort of constricting.

"Nothin' hurt," he told her. "It sure felt good bein' out an' around."

She put supper on the table. "Don't over-do it," she said. "Go slow, a little at a time."

He was beginning to be irritated. "I'll be careful." He changed the subject. "Mackensen — that's the settler's name — is startin' out like they all do, with big plans. He figures to build a barn."

Bessie put the whiskey bottle on the sideboard and sat down to supper. "What does his wife look like?"

"We never saw her. Or the children. They stayed in the house." Jawn Henry carved meat and salted it, never taking his eyes off the plate as he changed the subject again. "Looks like rain in a day or two."

Bessie ate for a while then said, "Do

they have chickens? Most squatters do."

"I heard chickens," Jawn Henry replied. "There was a sort of faggot fence, they was behind it."

"We could buy eggs from them," Bessie said, reaching for her coffee cup.

Jawn Henry filled his mouth which made it impossible to reply. By the time he had swallowed Bessie told him the doctor would be out from town tomorrow. She smiled across the table. "He'll be pleased you're doing so well, Jawn Henry."

Later, when Jawn Henry said he was tired and headed for the bedroom, Bessie followed. It was the first time they had shared their bed since last fall when Jawn Henry had been hurt and the doctor had told her to sleep in another room because Jawn Henry did not need being awakened by someone else pitching and tossing.

He was half asleep with Bessie beside him in the dark when she abruptly

50

said, "That little girl had eyes so blue they seemed almost violet. And pigtails like I wore when I was her age."

Jawn Henry considered, decided to feign sleep and breathed evenly and deeply. Bessie did not speak again.

In the morning when Jawn Henry took his hat off the peg in back of the kitchen door right after breakfast, Bessie got that stern expression on her face. "Talkin' sense to you, Jawn Henry, is sometimes about like talkin' to a rock. Just because you come through fine yesterday does not mean you can go back to actin' like you did before the accident. You remember that!"

He turned on her. "Gawddammit, I ain't a cripple an' I'm gettin' sick an' tired of you . . . "

Bessie's china blue eyes got moist, her mouth and chin quivered. Jawn Henry went around the table to her chair, leaving the hat on its peg. "All right, Bess. All right," he said in a

51

softer voice. "Tell you what — we could make up a hamper of meat an' biscuits like we used to do an' go up the creek to the cottonwoods. Would you like that?"

She smiled through unshed tears. "If you'll let me harness the horse and back her between the shafts when you hold them."

Jawn Henry lied with a good heart. "I was goin' to suggest that . . . I'll be right back. I got to tell Brad I won't be around much today."

He never did get his hat. He was reaching for it when she said, "Doctor Farrar . . . Remember? He said he'd be out today."

Jawn Henry's arm fell back to his side. "When's that old son of — ?"

"*Jawn Henry!* I don't know. All he said the last time he rode out was that he'd be back today."

They looked at each other until Jawn Henry returned to his chair and sank down. Bessie's eyes twinkled. Chagrin she understood very well without having heard that word to describe it. "We can have our picnic tomorrow. I'll fill your coffee cup," which she did, and sat back down across from him with her body between Jawn Henry and the bottle behind her on the sideboard.

Brad appeared on the porch. Bessie listened to her husband and softly smiled. Jawn Henry was a good man; she had known that before she had married him. Rough, irritable at times, but that seemed to go with this kind of a person.

He did not return right away so Bessie went about cleaning after breakfast. Once, she looked out. Jawn Henry was standing on the porch watching his riders leave the yard.

When he returned to the kitchen she said, "You get impatient. I understand that, but Jawn Henry because I love you, I don't want you to over-do an' be back down again."

He got a fresh cup of coffee, tipped whiskey into it when his wife appeared not to notice, and went out front under the overhang and sat in the same consarned chair he'd been sitting in every blessed day since last autumn, except for going buggy riding yesterday.

# 4

## Summer

FOR the most part folks in Templeton reacted in either one of two ways to Elias Farrar M.D. They were either respectful, awed and somewhat deferential, or, like Carney Witherspoon who owned the saloon, a rotund man with a fierce dragoon moustache to offset a lack of hair farther up, they were sullen around a tall, thin man who never smiled, always wore matching britches and coat, rarely visited the saloon and had never set foot in the card room, and who owned as nice a buggy mare as anyone had ever seen to pull his top-buggy with the especially built medicine cupboard below the dashboard.

Farrar had come to Templeton four years earlier from somewhere back east. He never said where and his bearing put off personal questions, not that it mattered. The people of Templeton, like the folks roundabout who had no other medicine man, passed their judgement on performance the same with the medicine man as with everyone else, and Doctor Farrar had accomplished some noteworthy cures.

Bessie Thomas was one who fell into the category who were impressed with Elias Farrar's education and bearing. But Bessie also respected preachers, and Templeton had gotten rid of two over the years, a priest who drank like a fish, and a minister who occasionally placed a hand on the legs of female congregationalists.

Bessie had the house spick-and-span before Jawn Henry's call from the porch that a buggy was easterly some distance. She changed her apron, plumped up her hair, made a final survey of the parlour then went out front, by which time Jawn Henry's eagle-like vision could identify the rig while it was about a mile out.

Bessie wanted to remind her husband to be civil and show respect, but one look at his profile told her it would be a waste of breath. Jawn Henry and Elias Farrar were flint on steel.

Shortly before the top-buggy entered the yard Jawn Henry went inside to the kitchen leaving the welcoming to his wife. He swallowed twice from the bottle kept discreetly far back in the dish cupboard, blew out a flammable breath, and returned to the porch as the rawboned tall man with the leathery unsmiling face was returning Bessie's greeting.

When Jawn Henry appeared the medicine man did not greet him, he instead studied him through slightly narrowed eyes and asked questions.

"How do you feel?"

"Fine."

"Have you been taking it easy?"

"Yes."

"Any pain in back down low?"

"No."

"How about your legs; get tired easily do they?"

Bessie saw the colour mounting and entered the conversation swiftly. "His legs was puny for a while, but now he's getting around pretty much like he used to . . . He and our rangeboss went buggy riding yesterday. He came back like he used to."

The doctor hooked both hands in the handle of his small leather satchel and regarded Jawn Henry. "It's taken a long time, and I'll admit I wasn't real hopeful. Not with a man whose life involves considerable physical effort. They usually don't do as I tell them. Well, Mister Thomas, I'm pleased. You should be too."

Bessie took them inside, seated them in the parlour and went to the kitchen to prepare the noon day meal. In her absence the two men sat eyeing each other. Jawn Henry asked how business was. Doctor Farrar recounted broken bones he had set, some cases of colic, an interesting delivery he had managed of a small woman whom he did not name, and ended up the recitation by saying he had cared for a broken hand for the new town marshal.

That, at least, interested Jawn Henry. He had not heard they had a new peace officer in Templeton. He asked first who the man was, and secondly how he had broken his hand.

Doctor Farrar answered the second question first. "He was breaking up a brawl in the roadway between two freighters . . . I didn't see the last part of it. I was told later that after the marshal hurled one man to the ground he turned and beat the other one badly, knocked him down, when the freighter got up onto all fours, he kicked him and when he fell the marshal picked him up, held him with one hand and beat him with the other hand."

"And broke his hand?"

"No. Mister Witherspoon from the saloon yelled for him to quit bloodying the half-conscious freighter. The marshal looked back at Mister Witherspoon, released his grip on the freighter, who fell in a heap . . . and a man came out of the crowd, tapped the marshal and when he turned, the man knocked him down.

"The marshal was arising as he reached for his holstered pistol when the other man grabbed him by the hair, hurled him sideways, got the gun, flung it away and waited for the marshal to get to his feet. The settler ducked under two blows and walked right into the third one . . . That is how the marshal broke his hand."

Jawn Henry leaned in his chair. "The settler . . . ?"

"I don't know him. Someone said he had a homestead northwest of town."

"What did he look like?"

"I told you, Mister Thomas, I did not see that part of the fight."

"So the marshal whipped him."

"No," the tall man replied. "The marshal broke his hand knocking the other man down, but according to folks who saw it, the settler jumped up and waded into the marshal, beat him to the ground and walked away."

Bessie spoke from the kitchen doorway. Jawn Henry followed their guest to the table. As they sat, heads bowed while Bessie asked the blessing Jawn Henry decided he would go to town at the first opportunity and see if his suspicion about that settler was correct.

Later, when Jawn Henry accompanied the medicine man to the barn, he asked the town marshal's name. Doctor Farrar was removing the nose bag from his buggy mare when he replied.

"Travis Carver. Folks called him Tex." The doctor was in the buggy evening up the lines when he also said, "Mister Carver went down-country for surgery on his hand. He left a note on the desk in his office with an address where the town council could send whatever wages was due him. He was not coming back."

Jawn Henry asked if the town council had hired a replacement. Doctor Farrar said he had no idea, nodded, backed his mare clear of the tie-rack, turned and drove out of the yard.

As events transpired Jawn Henry did not have to cover the six miles to Templeton to find an answer to his question.

When Brad arrived home just shy of sundown, riding a tired animal as were the other pair of rangemen, Bessie had come out front to summon her husband to supper and shared with Jawn Henry a quiet moment as they watched the hired hands swing off and lead their animals inside the barn to be cared for.

Bessie said, "What have they been doing? They look worn down."

Jawn Henry's answer was based on what he had mentioned earlier to the rangeboss. "Picked up some of Dobie's critters who was mixed in with ours and drove them back where they belonged."

"How did Dobie's animals get so far south, Jawn Henry?"

He held the door for her to precede

him inside as he mumbled something about cattle drifting when feed got short.

After supper while Bessie was tidying up, Jawn Henry went down to the bunkhouse. Only Brad was there, the other men were down at the creek taking an all-over bath.

The riders had eaten and cleaned up. Brad was sitting at the scarred old table in the centre of the room, his back to a large cast iron canon heater. He nodded a greeting to Jawn Henry and said, "We met Mackensen on our way back. He'd been cutting poles for his barn. He said to tell you he'd come by in the morning."

Jawn Henry sat down. "Did he say why?"

"He didn't say an' I didn't ask . . . We got Dobie's critters back on his range. There was one mottled cow as sly as they come. She'd managed to duck into every brush clump to hide. We spent almost as much time routing her out as we did making the drive . . . I wonder how them kids kept her going?"

Jawn Henry did not even guess about this. He told Holifield about a settler cleaning the plow of Templeton's new town marshal.

Brad's brow furrowed. "Mackensen?"

"The pill roller didn't know. I'll find out when he shows up tomorrow. I got to thinkin' this afternoon."

Brad half-nodded, eyeing Jawn Henry with a glint of irony in his eyes. "Might be favourable to us to sort of leave him alone."

Jawn Henry shrugged. "Part that. Part since we know he's good in a dog-fight, how good is he with a pistol?"

The other riders came in wearing only their long underwear. Sam Nesbitt nodded to Jawn Henry. The other rider, younger than anyone in the room, and evidently modest, put on his britches and boots. His name was Chester Bolling. He was called Chet, and stood at an even six feet with muscles packed well inside his hide.

He had dark hair and eyes and had looked to Jawn Henry when he had hired him to be maybe twenty-two or twenty-three.

Bolling was a quiet individual. The others talked, he listened. Brad had told Jawn Henry that Bolling was a good hand, but there were things he did not know, which made Brad wonder how long he had been rangeriding.

Jawn Henry drank a cup of vile coffee, visited for a while then returned to the main house. Bessie had left a parlour lamp lighted. She was already sleeping like the dead and did not even miss a breath when he climbed in beside her.

In the morning at breakfast he told her the squatter would be along and answered her mute look of enquiry with a shrug. "I got no idea."

"Maybe he wants work, Jawn Henry."

Her husband snorted. "We got all the hands we need, besides I doubt he knows one end of a cow from the other."

Bessie changed the subject. "That makes two town marshals that quit in a row." Her china-blue eyes came up to his face. "It wouldn't be *this* settler, would it?"

Jawn Henry was arising from the table when he answered. "I got no idea. I'll be down at the barn." When his wife's gaze swiftly arose to his face, Jawn Henry held up a hand. "I'm not goin' any further an' I won't lift anything."

Brad and the riders were gone as were fresh horses from the corral out back. Jawn Henry's restlessness had been increasing almost hourly since the buggy ride, and that stork with the little satchel who never smiled had not said Jawn Henry had to continue sitting on the porch.

In fact he had not even said he'd drive out again, which seemed to Jawn Henry to mean as far as the doctor was concerned, Jawn Henry was healed.

He was out back with a booted foot draped over the lowest stringer of the corral watching horses when he heard someone arrive out front.

It was getting hot and there was not a breath of air stirring. Jawn Henry walked up through the barn, met the settler on his combination horse, a good-looking animal weighing a tad over maybe nine hundred pounds, a sort of chestnut colour with an underlying hint of dapples. Unusual colour to Jawn Henry, who had thought he had seen them all during his lifetime.

Mackensen did not smile, he nodded and stated his purpose. "I got a little spare time, Mister Thomas, an' thought I'd ride over an', like I said, work out whatever I owe you for havin' to drive them cattle where my kids got them from."

Jawn Henry had not expected this, although if he had known Carl Mackensen better, he would have. He gestured, "Put your horse in a stall. I'll pitch him some feed, then we can talk."

Mackensen obeyed.

Jawn Henry was out front in humid warmth leaning on the tie-rack when the settler came out and leaned nearby. "You got a real nice place, Mister Thomas. Someday I'd like to have one, but that'll be down the road some years I expect."

Jawn Henry had been trying to think of work the settler could do. There was nothing requiring the kind of work a settler could do. In fact, not for another few months when he made his annual gather and drive to rails-end, all that was required on Cloverleaf was what his three riders could handle.

On the drive he could probably use another man, but that was some months away and the settler was in the yard as though he wanted to work now.

Jawn Henry shifted stance. "How are your children?" he asked.

Mackensen squinted a little when he replied. "You won't see hide nor hair of 'em over here again. An' they been cured of playin' cowboy."

Jawn Henry cleared his throat. "Brad said you was haulin' poles for the barn . . ."

Mackensen was still squinting into the distance. "It's a long haul, Mister Thomas. I stripped down the wagon, took a bed roll, food, and three axes. When I met Mister Holifield I was on my way home after four days of findin' the right trees, gettin' them down and loaded."

Jawn Henry knew something about that. The big barn behind them had taken him and a hired man all summer to put up.

"Did you finish digging that well?"

"No sir. I got too many distractions. But I'm down to gravel after goin' through six feet of chist."

Jawn Henry nodded. Chist in a dug well meant no water unless the digger kept on going. If he struck another strata of it he might as well quit.

"Gravel's promising," Jawn Henry said. "Moist gravel or dry gravel?"

"Dry. But it's down there."

Jawn Henry also gazed far out. He wanted to say "so is China." Instead he sighed and changed the subject. "This here is a hard land, Mister Mackensen. It don't give an inch. A man's got to buck everything from snow in winter to maybe drought or brush fires in summer."

Mackensen said something that made Jawn Henry laugh. "Mister Thomas this country makes it hard for a man to serve the Lord."

When Jawn Henry laughed the settler grinned. The ice was broken between them. Bessie, who had been watching from a window at the main house came to the edge of the covered porch and called that dinner was ready.

Mackensen straightened off the tie-rack. "About the work," he said.

Jawn Henry smiled. "I got a problem tradin' horses or sellin' cattle on an empty gut."

"Mister Thomas, I got to wash up . . . I really would like to settle about

70

the work an' get back home."

Jawn Henry nodded as though he hadn't been listening. "Out back's the trough."

They trooped through the barn. Mackensen rolled up his sleeves, washed noisily, faced Jawn Henry while combing his hair with crooked fingers. "I don't feel right about this," he said.

Jawn Henry studied the brawny younger man. "Can I ask where you're from, Mister Mackensen?"

"A little town north of Chicago. Why?"

"Well, y'see, out here we expect visitors to eat with us. It's custom. If I was over at your place I'd be put out if you didn't feed me."

Mackensen trooped toward the main house beside Jawn Henry. They hadn't quite reached the steps when he halted to speak. "By any chance are you friends to the town marshal at Templeton?"

"Nope. I didn't even know they had a new one until Doc Farrar told me yesterday. Why?"

"Well, if you had been, I would want to explain something to you before I set down to eat with you."

Jawn Henry's shrewd eyes were amused. "It *was* you that cleaned his plough."

"He was tryin' to beat that freighter to death. The man was out on his feet."

"You don't have to explain to me, Mister Mackensen. I didn't know that one . . . I knew the other one you run off, though. Not real well, just well enough to nod to. My opinion of that one was that he was too young for the job."

Bessie appeared in the doorway above the porch. Jawn Henry dutifully led off again.

Mackensen was embarrassed. Bessie talked about things in general, asked about his children, his wife, and mentioned something about buying eggs if the Mackensen's had any to spare.

Jawn Henry, a good feeder himself, was impressed with the amount of food the settler could put away, but he understood, years back when he had been engaged in considerable manual labour he ate like that too. A man had to, otherwise there wouldn't be any glue in his muscles when he used them.

As they were out front in the passing afternoon on the porch Bessie said if he'd send the children over with several dozen eggs she'd be obliged.

Mackensen smiled and nodded, then followed Jawn Henry to the barn where the best Jawn Henry could offer was employment as a hired rider when Cloverleaf made its annual drive down to the shipping pens.

Mackensen, instead of looking disappointed, seemed relieved. As he was riding out of the yard Jawn Henry went to lean on the tie-rack watching him go. With a barn to build, a well to dig, and chores that for most settlers seemed endless, the settler would have had to let things go at home that needed doing to fulfill his self-imposed obligation to Cloverleaf.

Jawn Henry went over and sat on the porch where Bessie joined him with a large pan to shell peas into. "Is he the one Doctor Farrar spoke about?"

"Yep. He is. You know why he come over? He figured he owed us for the trouble putting Dobie's cattle back where they belonged."

Jawn Henry did not see his mistake until Bessie raised china blue eyes. "Why would he owe us for Dobie's drift?"

Jawn Henry groaned to himself. "Well, because it was his children playin' cowboy who picked up some of Dobie's cattle an' drifted them among ours."

"You didn't tell me that, Jawn Henry."

"It didn't seem important . . . I'm goin' after a cup of coffee, want me to fetch you one?"

The china blue eyes were like ice

when Bessie shook her head without speaking and went back to shelling peas.

In the kitchen Jawn Henry laced his java, drank half of it and glared at his reflection in the kitchen mirror. Damned old fool, he silently told the reflection. You could have told her without letting on about hearing the children screaming as Mackensen took his belt to them.

# 5

## Town

JAWN HENRY wanted to go to town. When he had dusted his hat and was at the door, Bessie appeared wearing her special dress, the one with columbine or some kind of little blue flowers on it. She had her net bag and no hat. Bessie rarely wore hats. Her face was shiny, her eyes dancing.

Jawn Henry sighed inwardly. This was not to have been a social trip. Bessie turned completely around. "Do I look all right?" she asked, and he answered from the heart. "You always do, Bessie."

Well, so much for a few drinks with Carney Witherspoon and maybe a hand or two of stud. Neither of them had been to Templeton in better than six months, so they looked forward to it as he held the shafts and she backed the buggy animal between them, then elbowed him out of the way to do the harnessing.

The sky was dark, clouds were lying in wait over against the bow-shaped mountains. It was warm without any sunshine. Jawn Henry shook his head. He had rolled two ponchos and stowed them under the seat, which was the best folks could do when they didn't have enough sense to stay home with a storm hanging overhead.

It was cool, very pleasant during the drive. Summer heat or rain would punish them on the drive back, but as both understood from having lived long enough, the sweet parts of life and everyday existence, were followed by something different. Jawn Henry, as a male, accepted things as the cards fell without more than minimal grumbling, but his wife was more sensitive. It helped too that she had a sublimated variety of religion. To Bessie Thomas fate and God were interchangeable segments of the same thing; good went with bad. She knew this as surely as she knew there were miracles. Witness her husband's near brush with death last autumn or, at best, lifelong paralysis.

He had recovered.

They talked some on the drive to town, with long lapses of silence, which was another part of two people ideally mated; they did not have to talk, being together was enough.

Jawn Henry grunted at the sight of rooftops and trees. Templeton had grown a little over the years. Now, there were stores no one would have patronised when he had first come to the country. There was a dress shop, an apothecary shop, a land and abstract office — and a genuine medical doctor. Now there were also two churches, one, the Methodist church, had a peaked roof and a cupola with a cross atop it. The other, a Catholic church, had been made of stone to last a millenium, stained glass windows and a priest's residence under a huge old sycamore tree near the upper end of town.

As they drove past, the priest's housekeeper, an elderly woman with hair drawn severely back in a bun, was weeding a small flowerbed out front. She did not look up nor appear to hear the sounds of Templeton.

They left the rig in the care of a pimply-faced youth dressed in hand-me-downs who smiled and just naturally agreed with anyone older than he was, then parted out front, Bessie heading for the big general store which had oiled floors and the largest window in town of genuine, wavy glass.

Jawn Henry went up to the saloon, which, this time of day had few patrons, if one excluded four old gaffers dozing over near the unlighted stove.

Carney greeted Jawn Henry like a long lost brother. "I knew you got hurt last fall. Heard your back was broke or something like that. It's mighty good to see you, Jawn Henry. First drink's on the house."

There were two other customers at

the bar, faded-looking rangemen in need of a shearing and soap. Jawn Henry did not know them but when they nodded he nodded back. Carney set up the bottle and small jolt glass, and beamed. He was genuinely pleased to see Jawn Henry. "Hell, you look fine to me," he exclaimed. "Doc Farrar patch you up?"

Jawn Henry considered his reply carefully before giving it. "Well, danged horse run off a bluff with me. Killed the horse, which saved me the bother, cracked some bones in my back. Doc made me housebound for six months . . . Carney, you ever set on your butt for six months?"

As the barman shook his head Jawn Henry downed his jolt, breathed outward and continued with his recitation. "Set on the porch watchin' Brad and the other fellers ride out, and still be settin' there when they come back in the evening."

Carney smiled. "I expect a man'd have time to reflect on all the sins he done over his lifetime, wouldn't he?"

Jawn Henry returned the grin without answering. "One thing Farrar was good for, he brought the news from town, like that settler whupping the last marshal you had."

Carney's geniality vanished. He leaned on the bartop. "That son of a bitch. I was pullin' for him at first. There was two of them freighters, both big, stocky men. But after he put the first down out cold and went after the second one . . . Jawn Henry, he'd have killed that man. He never let him get up. He was down on all fours, head hanging, for all the world like a gut-shot bear. The marshal kicked him in the side, then stood him up with one hand and bloodied his face somethin' awful. I yelled for him to stop . . . A thick-built clod-hopper pushed through, knocked the marshal down, flung his sixgun away and jumped up after the marshal hit him, an' you never saw the like — he overhauled the marshal like a man killin' snakes with a short stick."

Jawn Henry knew all this. He was pouring his second jolt when Witherspoon concluded his recitation. "He done like the young marshal before him — he left town."

Jawn Henry turned the small glass in its own puddle as he said, "You know that settler, Carney?"

"No. Well, I know him on sight, but he's never been in here."

"Did you think he's the same feller who run off that big young feller before this last one? That young buck the town council hired after old man Crandal retired couple years back?"

Witherspoon's eyes widened. "I never heard that, Jawn Henry. You sure, because folks who seen that scrap never mentioned it was the same settler who whupped this last one."

"I'm sure," Jawn Henry said, and downed his whiskey. "His name's Mackensen. He's the squatter who bought railroad land adjoinin' my east line. Got a wife, two kids an' a potato patch out yonder."

"You know him?"

"Yes." Jawn Henry knew his limit so he placed some silver coins beside the sticky little glass and pushed the bottle aside as he asked if Templeton had replaced the latest lawman.

Because Carney had said the first drink was on the house he only took half the coins as he replied. "Nope. You know them dough-heads; they'll ponder and fiddle and put it off until folks get annoyed . . . Besides, I'm not sure any local fellers want the job."

There was a window-rattling clap of thunder. It seemed to come from directly above town. It came so suddenly, so loudly, so ominously that for some seconds folks were stunned, even frightened. As they were recovering another rattling noise erupted, this time not as loud and seemingly localised.

Another of those window-rattling rolls of overhead thunder erupted. The dozing old men over by the stove came wide awake and, like most other folks, hung still and hushed, shocked at the force of the thunder.

The last echo was dying when someone yelled. Jawn Henry swung toward the door. The old men did not move, still too shocked, and less able to react as instantaneously as Jawn Henry and Carney Witherspoon reacted. Both the rancher and saloonman burst past the spindle doors before the oldtimers struggled to arise.

Two bands of mounted men were reining around in obvious haste, one bunch was down at the general store, the second bunch was over in front of the brick bank building.

Jawn Henry's perception was swift. The man who had yelled had a harness shop south of the bank. He was out front in his brown apron as the first gunshot sounded. The men in front of the bank were spurring southward.

The harnessmaker went face down, dead before he hit the duckboards.

Carney Witherspoon gasped and raced back inside for his rifle. Jawn

Henry was not armed. Like most stockmen, wearing a heavy shellbelt and holstered sixgun was a nuisance. Most of the time anyway. He stood like a rock watching six hard-riders racing out of Templeton southward, low over their saddles, occasionally firing handguns.

Carney burst past his swinging doors with a Winchester rifle, not a carbine. He took long aim with a hand braced against an overhang upright, and fired. His was the only weapon fired until the outlaws were far enough southward to be out of handgun or carbine range. He levered up for another shot when the man at his side calmly said, "Too far, Carney."

Witherspoon fired anyway, then grounded his weapon as people emerged from stores, ganging together like mindless sheep. At the bank a thin man wearing black sleeve protectors appeared in the doorway. He did not make a sound, he simply stood there looking southward. Jawn Henry told

Carney he was going down to the emporium, his wife was down there. Carney nodded without taking his stare off the ant-sized horsemen speeding southward until that man across the way and slightly northward, slowly sank in the bank doorway. Carney started across the roadway as the first splash of raindrops as large as a spur rowel made dust jump upwards in the roadway.

Jawn Henry entered the store and stood dead still. The proprietor, a pasty-faced individual with a paunch who wore a massive gold chain across his lower vest, was on his knees with his back to the room. Jawn Henry looked for Bessie. Of the four customers, all women, in the store, there was no sign of his wife.

He started forward with a tight throat and an erratic heartbeat as Bessie appeared from a tiny office carrying a bottle of whiskey which she handed to the thick-bodied kneeling man.

Jawn Henry came up beside his wife, felt for her hand and held it tightly as he looked down where a youngish man with a bloody face and a ragged tear in the scalp was being fed whiskey, which he did not swallow and which made him cough and gag.

Jawn Henry leaned, took the bottle from the storekeeper and shook his head as he asked if the clerk had been shot.

Bessie answered. "One of them told the lad to give him two boxes of bullets, and when the clerk turned to obey, he was shaking like a leaf. The man with the gun hit him over the head. Hit him awfully hard, Jawn Henry."

A woman fainted very gently; she seemed to have known what was happening to her because she turned, reached slowly for the arm of another woman, missed the arm and sank very gently to the floor.

Two townsmen ran inside. Jawn Henry yelled for them to get Doctor Farrar. The second man, searching for his wife, answered as he recognized the fainted woman. "He ain't in town. Got

called out to some homesteader's place
. . . How is Howard? Chris'a'mighty, is
his skull busted? *Elizabeth!*"

The paunchy storekeeper arose
wagging his head. "Feels solid," he
said to no one in particular. "Couple
you lads lend me a hand. I got a cot
in the storeroom."

Jawn Henry led his wife outside. Up
in front of the bank there was a small
crowd. Jawn Henry took his wife to
the bench in front of the abstract land
office and sat down with her. Until she
was over there she had said nothing.
Now, her fingers in Jawn Henry's hand
began to squirm. He quietly said, "You
need a drink, Bess. I'll — "

"Don't leave me, Jawn Henry
. . . There were three of them, two
with beards one clean shaven. They
were dirty . . . I saw one of the bearded
ones hit that young man. I could hear
the sound." Bessie shuddered.

Jawn Henry's panacea for everything,
almost everything and that included
deep shock, was John Barleycorn.

Mostly he was not entirely wrong, but as Bessie began to shake, finally, he put an arm around her shoulders and pulled her head against him. He couldn't leave her.

Carney Witherspoon came southward without his rifle. He had tucked his apron under his belt. He was sweating, red-faced and wild-eyed. He stopped at sight of Bessie. "Is she hurt, Jawn Henry?" he asked between panting sounds from so much unusual activity.

"No, but she was in the store when they come. She saw one of them try to brain that young feller who works over there."

Carney sank down on the bench. "They killed Lionel Hardcastle. Right between the eyes. One shot. After the clerk come around he said Mister Hardcastle had opened the safe for them and was facing back around when the son of a bitch shot him in the face from a distance of about three feet.

"It's a mess in there. Blood, upended

chairs, papers flung every which way."

Jawn Henry had money in the bank. He and Mister Hardcastle had been friends of long-standing. He looked northward where several men were lifting the dead harness maker to take him inside.

Bessie spoke softly. "Jawn Henry, let's go home."

As he helped her arise those rowel-sized raindrops in the roadway were increasing the spurts of dust where they came down.

Jawn Henry held her around the shoulders, ignored the rainfall, found the livery barn empty, so he did the harnessing of the buggy animal, handed Bessie up, got in himself and drove into the alley, went northward until he found clear ground and headed due west.

The first couple of miles raindrops made the buggy-top shiny but had no effect upon the people below. Not until a low wind came did rain come inside. Jawn Henry looped the lines, dug out the ponchos, helped his wife get into one, put the other one on himself, unlooped the lines and talked up the buggy horse into a trot.

Raindrops increased in strength and came across the land in sheets of water, one directly behind the former ones. The buggy horse shook its head. There were not many things horses really disliked, but water in their ears was one of them. The horse lopped its ears downward as best it could, which helped, which would have been adequate except for wind-driven rain.

Jawn Henry knew his way home by heart. In fact he could have made the drive blindfolded, which is just about what his present situation amounted to. He could see the horse's head but no farther.

Bessie was inert at his side. For the first time anger stirred in him. By the time the horse, which knew its way home as well as its owner did, made a slow bending curve so as to enter the yard from the north, Jawn Henry's anger had turned cold and deadly. He had known the harness maker, not as well as he had known the banker, but he had liked the old man. He hadn't been armed when that son of a bitch on the running horse had shot him dead. He had been doing nothing more menacing than standing in front of his shop.

Lionel Hardcastle never wore a gun. He once told Jawn Henry he kept a sixgun in a desk drawer. He hadn't been at the desk. The ugly steel safe was across the room from the desk. Why was he shot dead after opening the safe so his bank could be raided? It didn't make sense.

The buggy horse walked into the barn without pressure on the lines to do so. It acted more relieved than it ordinarily did to stand still and drip water.

Jawn Henry climbed down. Bessie had not moved since the heart of the storm had arrived overhead. He freed the animal of the shafts, put it into a stall before pulling off the harness, forked feed into the manger, hurled the harness into the back of the rig and helped Bessie down. As they started for the main house the heavens opened up. Water came down without intermission. By the time they reached the covered porch both were soaked despite the ponchos.

Inside the house was dark, gloomy and cold. Jawn Henry made a fire, fed it until it burned fiercely, then got a glass of water, tipped whiskey into it and took it to his wife where she was sitting staring into the fire.

He handed her the glass, told her to drink it all down, which she did, although normally she never drank whiskey, did not even like the smell of it.

There were more rolls of thunder. Down at the bunkhouse feeble lamplight showed through the only window in the structure.

Jawn Henry fired up two lamps in the parlour and sat beside his wife to wait. It was not a very long wait. Bessie turned and said, "I never saw anyone killed before . . . He was a nice young man."

Jawn Henry patted her hand. "He wasn't killed. At least when we left he was still alive."

"But it was such a vicious, fierce blow, Jawn Henry." She returned her gaze to the fire. "It was so unnecessary."

Jawn Henry said, "Uh huh." He did not tell her right then that two men in town *had* been killed.

The rain sounded like thunder on the roof. As Jawn Henry sat gazing into the fire he had an errant thought. Rain was welcome; it made grass grow, but this was a gully-washer. Gully washers changed the configuration of the land. They made deep arroyos where only slight depressions had been, and if they were accompanied by strong winds, they bowled over huge trees, tore roofs off, set animals to drifting heads down, rumps to the force.

# 6

## A Wagon Ride

EVERYTHING in the Templeton countryside was sublimated to the storm, including two murders and two robberies. The storm passed after two days, the sky showed azure blue, the sun was warm again. It made steam rise from the sodden countryside. But traffic, foot or horseback, was limited for another few days until the ground firmed up enough to be ridden over.

The last day of the storm Jawn Henry went down to the bunkhouse. Brad, Sam Nesbitt and Chet Bolling listened to Jawn Henry in shocked silence. Brad made a revealing comment afterwards. He said, "That was foolish. Where could they go in the storm? You can't run a horse very far when mud's caking on his fetlocks an' the ground's as slippery as grease."

Templeton had no telegraph. Despite its recent growth no wires had been strung to town yet. Sam Nesbitt gave the result of his pondering. "Mud or no mud, they sure as hell sent someone east to Downieville to the telegraph."

As usual the muscular, large youngster among them said nothing. He shoved wood into the stove, hefted the speckleware coffee pot and went around topping up their cups.

Brad sighed and wagged his head. He had known the harness maker fairly well. He seemed to be mourning the old man's passing although he said very little about it. Sam was still pondering about the outlaws. The nearest town south of Templeton was down at a place called Exeter. Which was where the shipping corrals and railroad yards were. The distance from Templeton to Exeter was about sixty miles. Sam rolled a smoke with pensive deliberation, fired it over the lamp mantle, blew smoke and said, "Ain't nothin' but open country an' a few cow outfits between Templeton an' Exeter. In this kind of a storm where could six men find shelter? An' their horses would suffer. An outlaw on a wore-down horse gettin' half-drowned in a gully-washer, hadn't ought to be too hard to find, had he?"

"Six of them," Jawn Henry stated, and leaned as though to arise. "They wouldn't be hard to find except for the same damned mud and punishment possemen would have, an' with no lawman in Templeton, an' I'd guess not too many men willing to go after them during the storm . . . An' somethin' else: Now there won't be any tracks to follow."

The following day when the sun shone Jawn Henry's riders fed, used sticks to un-clog their boots, and puttered. Sam and Chet jacked the wagons and the light rig off the ground, removed each set of wheels, slathered grease, made sure the leather retainers

97

were still serviceable, and patched a little harness.

Brad worked on some notes he'd taken over the last few weeks; estimated steers big and heavy enough to be trailed down yonder, tallied the carcasses they had found of dead animals, mostly old gummer cows, and added that number to the number of heifers that should be kept back as replacements.

The third day, when it was possible to cross the yard without ending up with a couple of pounds of mud adhering to a man's boots, they all rode out. Bessie did not say anything as Jawn Henry went down to rig out with the riders, but she watched from the window as he and the others left the yard.

She had not slept well since the ruckus in town. She awakened in full darkness seeing the store clerk bloody and senseless on the floor.

Her late father had told her — not once but at least five times — about the time two outlaws had robbed the store. That had been back when old

Carver the town marshal had been in his prime. He took an Indian and the blacksmith, rode those men down, killed them both and returned with them tied across their saddles. She had not seen the dead men.

They were buried quickly. Her father got back the two hundred and seventy dollars the outlaws had stolen.

She distinctly remembered her father's summation of that episode. He had said, "Back east the marshal would have caught hell for what he did. Thank gawd out here we know the difference between justice and the law."

She went to the garden patch, stood considering the small plants that had their roots exposed and the larger ones that had been beaten to the ground. With nothing better to do and in order to give her hands something to do she re-planted the small plants and tied the flattened ones to stakes she pounded into the ground. Her loss would probably be considerable. Something occurred to her Jawn Henry had once said. The trick in this life is to take maybe three steps forward so that when disaster strikes and destroys things you lose one step — and are still two steps ahead.

That evening after Jawn Henry had cleaned up and came to the kitchen to visit while Bessie made supper, his gaze was bright, there was good colour in his face and although Bessie wanted to ask about his back, she decided that since he was in such good humour it must not be bothering him. Besides, he had been getting increasingly irritable when she worried aloud.

She broke stride at the stove to fill a cup with black coffee, leaving a couple of inches for the whiskey he tipped in. He watched her the way one mate does another, and eventually said, "Don't think on it, Bess. Things like that lead to a broodin' temperment."

She smiled at him and worked in silence. But as she was placing their plates of food on the table she said, "I wonder about the store clerk."

Jawn Henry drained the coffee cup before speaking. "I'll send Sam to town in the morning to find out how he come out . . . An' to learn what's bein' done to catch those — "

"*Jawn Henry!*"

He got his own re-fill at the stove and returned to the chair. Bessie mentioned something her husband had not considered. She said, "Doctor Farrar will mend him if it can be done."

Jawn Henry nodded, ate, and eventually pushed the empty plate aside to lean both elbows atop the table gazing over at her. "We had a little drift in the direction of Mackensen's darned spud patch. Lucky we found them before they got any closer."

"You drifted them back?"

"Yes. Took most of the afternoon. We put 'em so far off they'll be a week goin' back, if they try it."

"Why don't he fence his potatoes?"

Jawn Henry did not answer the question, his mind was fully occupied

101

with something else. "There wasn't no fire from the chimney."

"Maybe they didn't need one."

Jawn Henry's brows settled in a faint frown. "After that storm everyone needs to dry out from inside. Sod houses like his get soaked clean through. It takes a hot fire to get 'em dry again. It takes days."

Bessie went after her second cup of coffee and while at the stove she said, "Did you ride on in?"

"No. It was gettin' along an' we wanted to push the cattle a long ways." He waited until she was seated at the table again before saying more. "We could hear the chickens caterwaulin' to high heaven. Chet said when his maw's chickens done that they were hungry."

Bessie's very blue eyes came up to her husband's face. She did not say a word. Jawn Henry considered the black contents of the cup in front of him. "Maybe they went visitin' before the storm an' haven't got back yet."

Bessie leaned on the table without taking her eyes off her husband. Jawn Henry fidgeted, he knew that look, had seen it often enough over the years. "I'll ride over tomorrow."

"It could be they're all down with the croup, Jawn Henry."

He nodded.

She spoke again, quietly. "I want you to do something for me." That approach never failed and she knew it.

"All right. What?"

"If they're sick fetch the youngsters back with you. A sick mother can't look after them."

He returned her stare and smiled a little. "I'll take the buggy."

" . . . And if Mister Mackensen an' his wife are down . . . "

"I'll take the spring wagon."

She smiled at him. "I'll have things ready when you get back." She took his cup to the sideboard, spilled a tad of whiskey into it, topped it up from the coffee pot and placed the cup in front of him with a twinkle.

In the morning with firmer ground underfoot Brad harnessed the team for Jawn Henry and stood back as his employer climbed from the hub to the seat. As Jawn Henry was evening up the lines Brad said, "I finished tallyin' yesterday. Sam an' Chet are goin' south to bring back any drift the storm caused . . . If you didn't care I could ride along with you."

Jawn Henry slapped the board beside him. Brad got up there and Jawn Henry talked up the team.

The sun was warm; it probably would get even warmer later in the day although there was still considerable moisture in the world.

There were larks in the recovering grass, one little puffy white cloud floated sedately overhead, otherwise the heavens were clear and brilliant blue, almost the colour of turquoise.

Brad got his first cud of the day settled, spat over the side once then settled back to relax and watch for chuck holes and creases in the range that had become miniature canyons. Jawn Henry watched too. Several times he sashayed out and around.

By the time they could see the Mackensen place with its low-profiled half sod house, the heat had increased a little. Brad sat forward. Four horses were standing hip-shot in the sunshine. When they heard the wagon they raised their heads and nickered. Neither Brad nor Jawn Henry commented; there was no need. Lifelong horsemen knew when horses were hungry and had not been fed.

Jawn Henry skirted the spud patch and shook his head. The storm had not only torn the ground to expose roots, it had also pounded flat the shoots. If Mackensen got potatoes from that planting, it would be maybe just barely enough for his family with none to peddle in town.

He drew line in the yard, hooked the binder with a booted foot, looped the lines around the binder handle and sat there. Brad was still too. Whether folks believed or not, and most did not, there were times when a man could sit still and pick up something, maybe with his brain, maybe with his heart, that warned him. It was no more than a hint, but it was real.

Brad stirred first. He climbed down on the off side, dropped the tether weight from under the seat and hooked it. Jawn Henry only glanced at the rangeboss before he also climbed down. He walked to the head of the hitch and called the settler's name.

A hungry horse nickered otherwise there was silence. He called again. Brad brushed Jawn Henry's sleeve with a gloved hand. "Door's part open."

The closer they got to the house the stronger became that strange feeling. They could see very little past the door. Jawn Henry called again, not as loud this time. Brad reached to gently push the door open wider. Inside the soddy had light shining against one window of scraped rawhide.

Brad let his breath out slowly. "Gawd a'mighty."

Mackensen was face down in a pool of blood. The back of his shirt where he had been shot showed scorch. The killer had been very close when he fired.

The drab woman was half off, half on a sort of trundle bed that had been built against the west wall below the window. She had been shot twice, once through the shoulder, the next time through the centre of the chest. Her face had a look of congealed terror frozen in place.

There were flies buzzing. Jawn Henry toed Mackensen onto his back, his expression reflected surprise. The bullet that had exited in front had come out above his heart. He had evidently been shot while either arising or while he was bent over.

Brad slowly removed his riders' gloves, tucked them under his belt and pointed to a shellbelt and empty holster hanging from a wooden peg.

Jawn Henry had already seen those things. He softly said, "It's not here. If he'd got hold of it . . . Brad whoever done this took the gun with him."

Brad removed his hat to swipe sweat off with a cuff before replacing the hat. "Why? For Chris'sake, why? Not for his horses, they're outside, an' no one'd believe a settler's got money."

Jawn Henry went back to stand in the doorway with heat on his back. His gaze moved slowly and settled again on the dead settler. He had looked once at the woman and could not do that again. He said, "Them boxes nailed to the wall been emptied."

Brad crossed to look. There was one dented can of peaches lying near the cold stove. It looked like someone had stumbled over it, or maybe had stepped on it. Otherwise all the bottles the woman had put up and the tinned goods put aside for winter, were gone.

The bedding had been ransacked. Hooks where two weapons had been were empty. Jawn Henry said, "He had a shotgun?"

"Yes. An' a Winchester rifle."

"The son of a bitch took them too."

Jawn Henry twisted to gaze out where the horses stood, heads high, watching the men at the house. His initial shock had passed. "Well now," he mused aloud more to himself than to his rangeboss. "Why didn't the son of a bitch take a fresh horse?"

Brad shouldered past into sunlight, stood a moment then pointed. "It wasn't a 'him', Jawn Henry. Look at them tracks."

For a long time they studied the soft earth before Jawn Henry went over to lean on the wagon as he said, "Brad . . . ?"

"Yeah. I'm thinkin' the same thing, Jawn Henry. Them murdering bastards didn't continue on southward, they cut back an' come up here. That looks to me like shod horses. What does it look like to you?"

Jawn Henry studied the ground over

a long period of quiet before he looked up and spoke. "My guess is that the lads in town are boilin' out all over the countryside — southward . . . Well, it's early, the ground's soft enough; somewhere around here there's got to be diggin' tools."

This time, when Jawn Henry had been at it more than an hour, his back hurt. He stubbornly kept on digging, lips pressed flat, eyes on the ground, until Brad paused to rest, leaned on his shovel and said, "Jawn Henry, go set in the wagon."

"I'm fine. We're about through anyway."

Brad did not yield an inch. "If I bring you back walkin' humped over and in pain, you got any idea what Bessie's going to do? She won't speak to me for a year — maybe longer . . . Jawn Henry — *please* — go set in the wagon."

"Brad, somethin' is botherin' me."
"Your back. If you don't go set in the — "

"Where are the children?"

Brad closed his mouth, regarded his employer for a moment before craning around as he said, "For a damned fact — where are they? You don't suppose them sons of — ?"

"Why would they take little kids? Maybe they're hid somewhere. Sure as hell they wasn't in the house or they'd be dead too."

Brad went to work filling in the last grave. "I'll be along directly. See if you can find 'em. You know their names? Maybe if you called . . . "

Jawn Henry left his shovel where it fell and called. He did not know the name of Mackensen's children, was sure he'd never heard it, but he walked out and around calling to them, identifying himself and telling them it was safe to come out, wherever they were.

The only response he got was the four horses, startled by the shouting ran off with the bay horse in the lead.

Brad finished mounding the second

grave, started to pull on his riders' gloves and winced. He had two blisters large enough to notice. He finished pulling on the gloves and joined Jawn Henry beating the brush. They did not find the children even after they were in the wagon so they could widen the scope of their search.

They gave up as the sun sank. Now, they would not get home until 'way late, nor did they talk much on the drive. Once, Brad said, "They'll be all right. Night's are warm now."

The reply he got was bleak. "Tomorrow all four of us will come over here, find their tracks and round them up. I don't think they'll go back into that house. Even if they did there's only that can of peaches. We'll find them Brad."

The rangeboss nodded. Neither he nor Jawn Henry knew they would not find the children, someone else would.

# 7

## On Firm Ground

JAWN HENRY'S back ached for a fact but that wasn't what made his steps lag on the way to the main house from the barn where Brad was caring for the horse and wagon.

Bessie had seen them coming and was standing in the doorway. He did not have to say anything. At first she thought it was his back, closer to the porch he got and the better she could see his face, she knew it wasn't his back and her heart stopped for one second.

He herded her back inside, got some whiskey in a cup of cold coffee, sat down in the parlour with a long sigh, and told her what they had found over yonder and what had taken them so long.

He hadn't wanted to tell her. On the

drive back he groaned inwardly over what lay ahead. She was still moping about that store clerk.

She got white to the hairline, her china blue eyes looked through and past Jawn Henry. She clasped and unclasped her fingers. Eventually in a voice little stronger than a whisper she said, "The children too?"

Jawn Henry emptied the cup. It never made any difference to him whether coffee was hot or cold, only that it was tart and wet.

"No, they wasn't around. I called. Brad and me drove through the brush. No sign of them."

" . . . How long ago did it happen?"

Jawn Henry studied the inside of the empty cup. "I'd say the day after the storm. Maybe when the rain was taperin' off because there was shod horse tracks. There was six of them, Bessie. Same number as raided Templeton. Brad figures it was the same men."

Bessie wasn't interested in the outlaws.

"Those children was out in the rain. They'll have caught the fever by now. Jawn Henry . . . !"

"Bess; we'll find them. I an' the riders'll comb the damned countryside. They're small an' short-legged. They can't have got far."

"Maybe they headed for Templeton."

He conceded that, but doubted it. "Maybe. One thing's sure, we'll pick up their tracks."

"Or find them half sick to death."

"No, damnit," Jawn Henry exclaimed, recognising the mood that was beginning to clutch his wife. "Hungry, scairt peeless and wanderin' around, but with the sun hot again — "

His wife jumped up. "I'll start supper." She whisked past him with frantic haste. He sat a while, then for no reason except long habit, he skived kindling, fed wood in until a healthy fire was burning, then stood back holding the empty cup thinking about the country he thought the Mackensen children had fled over.

Tracks. In the morning he and the riders would spread out. There would be small foot-tracks. That was the only good thing he could think of that had come out of that damned gully-washer.

He thought he heard riders down by the barn, but maybe not, the fire was crackling and Bessie was rattling pans in the kitchen. Anyway, if it was riders it would be Sam and Chet coming back from hunting a drift southward. He abruptly straightened up. He had told Bessie he'd send Sam to town and had plumb forgot it.

Well, he wouldn't send him tomorrow. The folks in Templeton could hang and rattle, right now they had to find two terrifed children who had most likely lost their way in the storm . . . Most likely, too Bessie was right about them catching their death during the downpour, but he would not think on that let alone say anything about it.

Bessie was in the doorway to call

116

Jawn Henry to supper when a heavy gloved fist rattled the front door. Bessie gave a little start. That hadn't been a knock it had been a pounding.

Jawn Henry parked the cup and went scowling to open the door. He stopped dead in his tracks and behind him across the parlour Bessie gasped. Sam Nesbitt had one child by the hand and another one in his arm part way over his shoulder.

He walked in, made straight for the fire, held the little girl with both arms and gently shoved the little boy closer to the fire.

Both children were filthy, their clothing was torn, there was blood from scratches, their faces were stone set in identical expressions of terror and something else just below the surface.

Sam said, "Chet an' me was makin' a circle around to leave the drift up yonder a mile or so northward . . . there they was, the little boy standing rigid, the little girl on the ground. Ma'm, she's sick."

117

Bessie rushed forward, took the girl in her arms and fled toward a bedroom in the rear of the house.

Jawn Henry looked at the boy. His eyes were unwilling to return Jawn Henry's gaze, even after the older man asked his name and he answered.

"Axel . . . Mackensen." The dry stare remained. "Our paw an' maw . . . Some men come durin' the storm an' killed them. Belinda and me was at the leanto to fetch some stove wood . . . " The boy's gaze went slowly to Sam Nesbitt. The older squinty-eyed man smiled, gently patted the boy's head and Axel Mackensen grabbed Sam's leg with both arms and made muffled half screams, half choking sobs.

Sam was embarrassed and raised his eyes to Jawn Henry. "He's starved and barely dry yet, but *her*, she sounds like a horse with distemper. That one's sick."

Jawn Henry went to the kitchen with Sam Nesbitt. His limited experience in kitchens did not go much beyond making beef broth, and since the stove was still hot as he chopped meat to put into the boiling water he told Nesbitt what he and Brad had found at the Mackensen place.

The rangeman sat down, studied his work-roughened hands and did not say a word until Jawn Henry had the mug of hot broth for the lad, then, as Jawn Henry started back to the parlour, the rangeman softly said, "Good trackin' weather. Chet an' me hardly had any trouble at all . . . Was they ridin' shod horses?"

"Yes. You tell Brad first thing, we all go scoutin' from the Mackensen place until we find their sign."

"You want me to leave the boy here?"

Jawn Henry turned with a testy glare, but bit back the sharp retort to say, "Yes. My missus an' I'll look after them."

When Nesbitt got back to the bunkhouse he could tell by the look on Chet's face that Brad had told him what he and Jawn Henry had found, and had done, at the settler's place.

For awhile the powerfully-built younger man sat absorbing heat from the canon heater. None of them were very talkative, but later, as young Bolling got to his feet he said, "I understand why they'd cut back after folks saw 'em leave town southward — to throw off anyone who come after them. But why kill them two folks they didn't even know, if all they wanted was grub?"

Sam's pithy opinion offered no clue about that, but his profanity left no doubt about his reaction. It had been a long day for all of them. Long after the light had been doused at the bunkhouse two lamps still burned at the main house.

Jawn Henry was dead to the world but Bessie was up and down most of the night. The next morning as Jawn Henry was dressing his wife said she thought the girl had developed a lung complaint, that if the child wasn't so sick she'd hitch up the buggy and take her to town to see Doctor Farrar.

Jawn Henry said nothing until after he had breakfast, then he went to look for a light at the bunkhouse. It glowed so he returned to the kitchen. "Keep her warm, Bess. I'll send Chet for Farrar."

For the first time in ages Jawn Henry buckled his shellbelt and holstered Colt into place, pecked his wife's cheek and left.

At the barn there were a few short morning greetings. It was darker than the inside of a hat. Everyone'd had coffee and breakfast but those things which normally brightened the spirits of even the sourest of men, had made no effect.

Jawn Henry told the big young rangeman to fetch that danged stringbean of a medicine man back for the Mackensen girl, if he had to use a gun to do it.

Sam, Brad and Jawn Henry rode straight up buttoned to the gullet. It was cold as well as dark. They were in no hurry since tracking required sunlight. Sam Nesbit made the air fragrant with his first smoke of the day, and made an observation about how far out of the country the outlaws could be with so big a head start. Neither Brad nor Jawn Henry commented because as they neared the settler's place the sun was rising and they were watching the ground.

Tracks of six shod horses left the yard, skirted the barnpoles that had been set on saw horses to be draw-knifed, also went around the mound of dirt where the well-hole was, then went northeast as straight as six arrows.

Nesbitt said no more about the time that had lapsed between the murders and now, but he stood in his stirrups every now and then to scan ahead. The air was as clear as glass, the sun climbed, but without heat until mid-morning. The horses hiked along until Jawn Henry boosted his animal into a slow lope and held him to it for better than a mile with Brad and Sam following.

The farther Jawn Henry rode the more he wondered if they hadn't ought to figure some quicker way to catch up, maybe stop a stage and travel that way, which would make better time unless the tracks veered, in which case they'd be going merrily northeast and the outlaws would be going in some other direction.

But Jawn Henry knew one thing for a damned fact, because in his time he had ridden with his share of possees: As long as riders were behind someone who had a decent head start, they would always be where the outlaws had *been*, never up where they *were*. When he mentioned this during one of the spells when they walked the animals to rest them, Brad said, "It ain't a horse race, Jawn Henry, it's a *man* race. We can get horses as we go along, but the three of us don't dare give out, an' somewhere down the pike we'll find them."

They rode with the sun high and tracks setting up firm as the earth got harder. It was the easiest tracking any of them had ever done.

Brad settled a cud into his cheek, eyed the position of the sun and dryly said, "It can go down any time it wants, we keep riding. Tonight, tomorrow, tomorrow night. Somewhere there'll be a ranch with fresh horses."

Sam Nesbit was not convinced. "They don't know we're back here, so they'll rest. After all, they put in some hard ridin' during some real bad weather. Either them or their horses got to stop somewhere."

Brad made another dry remark. "Unless they get fresh horses too."

Sam said no more. That thought had not occurred to him and he did not like it. But the more he thought about it the more he remained certain that whether the murderers got fresh horses or not, they, themselves, would require a time to let down, especially since they did not know three *vengadors* as the Mexes

124

said, were grimly in pursuit.

And something else did occur to Sam Nesbitt. "The odds ain't too good."

Jawn Henry who had taken no part in the discussion up to now, commented without looking away from some timbered country they were approaching — perfect bushwhacking country. He said, "Men like this bunch will raid again, maybe take over some isolated cow camp or something. They got to get fresh animals, an' they ain't made of iron either. If they come across some outfit that don't look too tough . . . Hell, they shot up the Mackensen place didn't they?"

Sam agreed. "Yeah. I guess so . . . What sticks in my craw is why? They took no horses, sod-busters never have money . . . "

The same thing had stumped his companions but neither of them took up the discussion; they were approaching timber with darkness past the first ranks of huge firs and pines. Jawn Henry gestured. "Split off, it's maybe nothin' but if they're waitin' in there an' we ride bunched up . . . "

Sam went south, Brad went north. Jawn Henry rode straight toward the trees. They had been seen for a fact, it wasn't possible for riders, or men afoot for that matter, to enter a bosque of trees without a dozen set of eyes noticing and watching. But they had four legs, not two.

There was nothing wrong with caution, in fact under the circumstances it was commendable. But they rode slowly into the timber, through it and out the other side without encountering anything except the tracks they had been following for miles.

Jawn Henry stopped still in timber gloom to study the sunbright rolling land beyond. When Brad and Sam came up he pointed toward what looked like a set of big square rocks, except that smoke was rising from the top of the biggest one.

They sat, looked, estimated the distance to be as much as maybe two miles. Brad looked down. The tracks led straight toward that rising smoke, all of it across open country.

Jawn Henry looked for more trees. There was a thick stand of them northward, all the way atop a rocky escarpment but there were no trees anywhere else.

The moment three riders appeared in broad daylight, anyone over yonder where the smoke was rising would see them — if someone was looking. But even if no one was looking when they left cover, sure as hell was hot they would see three riders crossing the couple or so miles that would be required to approach that ranch, or whatever it was. A walking horse makes good time at four miles an hour. Two miles a half hour.

Brad was gnawing off a fresh cud when he spoke around it. "We got two choices; set right here until dark and those bastards will get that much farther ahead again, or ride maybe miles out of our way through the trees

127

an' come down closer to the yard with late-day shadows to help."

Jawn Henry dismounted to rest his horse's back. Sam and Brad did the same. It was squinty-eyed Sam Nesbitt who detected a mob of horsemen coming up-country from the south as though they might have come from Templeton. There were too many for it to be riders for that distant ranch. Brad thought there was about fifteen of them.

Jawn Henry made a guess. "Possemen from town."

Sam doubted that. "Why up here if them bastards left sign southward?"

Jawn Henry did not answer. The three of them stood at the head of their animals watching and saying nothing until Nesbitt's screwed-up eyes picked out something else. He twisted and pointed. There were two horsemen atop the rocky escarpment at the east end of the trees. They were sitting their saddles like Indians, looking in the direction of the grey-rising smoke and, southward, at that band of horsemen.

Not a one of them had an explanation to offer for those two riders backgrounded by big trees on the topout.

Jawn Henry swore under his breath. They were wasting time. One thing was clear; whoever that big band of horsemen were, if they were unfriendly and the three Cloverleaf riders went down toward them . . . Jawn Henry swore again, snugged his cinch, swung over leather and reined in and out among the big trees where they would not be noticeable to the large party of other riders, picking his way toward the other two up there watching eastward. At least they out-numbered those two.

They were wasting time no matter what they did, since they could not follow the easterly tracks, and that did little for their dispositions. They had now been a-horseback since before daylight, and while hunger was present among them, it had been present with each one of them dozens of times, they had learned long ago to live with postponing a meal or two, but after making such good time tracking, and with some reason to suspect they might, if they rode all night and the next day, pick up some indication of the whereabouts of their outlaws, it irritated the hell out of all three of them to be halted now.

For that reason as they picked their way in the direction of the pair of statue-like riders on the rocky hilltop with trees and their litter to mask their approach, none of them was in a charitable mood.

Jawn Henry halted, swung off, tied his horse and resumed the stalk on foot. Sam and Brad followed, and they at least had carbines. All Jawn Henry had brought was his belt gun.

Men whose lives and livelihood were spent on horseback made poor hikers, especially in rocky country, uphill all the way.

They stopped twice to 'blow'. The last time Brad shook his head and spoke softly. "They been sittin' up there like scoutin In'ians for a damned hour."

Jawn Henry had no quarrel with that. In fact he was grateful they hadn't moved as he started forward again, this time tugging loose the tie-down thong that kept his sixgun securely in its holster. As he did this Sam and Brad held their carbines crossways in both hands during the final climb.

Where they halted, sucking air, they were less than a hundred feet behind the pair of motionless horsemen. Jawn Henry crept closer, halted and cocked his Colt.

The pair of horsemen became rigid. They could for a fact have been carved from stone. Jawn Henry slipped closer, halted, scowled and lowered the cocked pistol as he said, "Dobie! What in the hell are you doin' this far from home?"

The elder of the horsemen craned around. He was thick with a paunch that filled the part of a saddle with an eighteen-inch seat that his normal saddle parts did not fill.

He had a squeaky voice when he said, "For Chris'sake Jawn Henry. You liked to scairt the waddin' out of me."

# 8

## Complications

DOUGHBELLY PIERCE'S companion was a bronzed, hawk-nosed man with coal black hair and eyes to match, who barely nodded when Dobie introduced him to Jawn Henry Thomas.

"His name's Horn Thompson." Doughbelly paused. "Name's really Leghorn Thompson. You ever hear someone namin' a kid after a chicken before?"

Leghorn Thompson's black gaze was fixed unblinkingly on Dobie Pierce. Jawn Henry did not comment. He asked again what his neighbour with the 'possum gut was doing this far from his home place.

The answer did not come from Dobie, it came from his companion, who was back watching the activity far ahead.

"Them fellers who shot up Templeton, killed the banker an' an old man, are supposed to be at that ranch you can make out from here."

Jawn Henry looked at the dark man. "Who says they're over yonder?"

Leghorn Thompson turned his head slowly, examined Jawn Henry, Brad and Sam before returning his black stare to Jawn Henry. "I say they're over there. Leastways when I left Templeton last night headin' home, the information I had was that someone had seen them ridin' up-country east of your yard some distance, heading northeasterly." Before Jawn Henry could ask who had told Leghorn Thompson that, someone a long way off fired a gun. After a moment another gun was fired, this time it was unmistakably a shotgun because both barrels cut loose. That kind of a noise travelled a long way.

When silence returned Jawn Henry asked Dobie if he knew who that big party of riders belonged to, and again the black-eyed man answered. "That's what we was wonderin' about when you come along, Mister Thomas. I figure the news of them renegades headin' up this way instead of southward, got spread, an' what you see is the result. Riders from Templeton."

Dobie nodded his head and resumed looking across the open country. Jawn Henry turned, met the eyes of his companions and faintly shrugged before facing Doughbelly again. "Have you got some notion in mind? That's an awful lot of open country if Mister Thompson's wrong an' those aren't men from town."

Pierce had no plan. "You seen us arrive over here. We don't know any more'n you do . . . Jawn Henry, how come you to be this far from home?"

Jawn Henry explained. The longer he talked the more interest Leghorn Thompson showed in what he said, until the dark man asked a question as Jawn Henry wound down.

"The children too?"

"No. Sam here found them. My wife's lookin' after them at home."

Jawn Henry's eyes widened a little. "You knew the Mackensens? You knew they had kids?"

Leghorn Thompson shifted in the saddle. His horse had to adjust to the re-distribution of weight and Sam Nesbitt, whose annoyance had been growing, said, "Why don't you fellers get off them horses. A horse standin' still ain't a chair."

Doughbelly looked startled and jumped his gaze from Nesbitt to Leghorn Thompson, who was looking steadily at Sam without speaking or moving. Jawn Henry wasn't sure he had ever before seen anyone whose face looked menacing even when it had no particular expression. It dawned on him why Dobie Pierce deferred to the hawk-faced dark man. Jawn Henry wondered just who Leghorn Thompson was and why he was over here with Doughbelly Pierce.

When the dark man leaned forward before dismounting he ignored Nesbitt and answered Jawn Henry's question.

"Carl Mackensen an' I was cousins. He wrote me last winter to come out an' see the country. I came out this spring."

"Did you see your cousin?"

"No. I hunted for work first an' hired on with Mister Pierce. I was goin' to look him up." The obsidian eyes turned toward Jawn Henry and remained there. If Leghorn Thompson had been shocked to learn of the murder of his cousin he did not show it. But the next thing he said suggested that he was surprised — and that he was something else.

"I guess I shouldn't be surprised. Mister Pierce's range bein' north of Cloverleaf, him an' me struck out due east. Once, we cut sign of shod horses, looked like six of them, an' directly we come out on this point among the trees . . . I'm goin' down there. By any chance would you know which of them six killed Carl an' his wife?"

Jawn Henry shook his head. Leghorn Thompson raised his left hand with the reins in it, nodded and started to move when Doughbelly stopped him. "There's a regular darned army down there, Horn."

The dark man's reply was cryptic. "Sure looks like it, didn't it?"

Brad blew out a long breath as they watched Leghorn Thompson skirt along the spit of timber in the direction of that distant ranch. Brad said, "Jawn Henry . . . ?"

For a way there was timber cover, but it trickled down to buckbrush and red-barked manzanita which was not always tall enough to conceal moving horsemen.

Jawn Henry grunted and started back where they had left the horses. Nobody heeded Doughbelly, but he struck out in the wake of his hired rider.

When the Cloverleaf men caught up, Dobie Pierce was a good hundred yards behind Thompson, and even though the cover for that far, and somewhat farther, was adequate, Jawn Henry and his companions got the impression that Dobie was not trying to catch up with the dark-eyed man.

Thompson's full attention was up ahead where sunshine showed roiled dust but there was no more gunfire. Jawn Henry waited for a wide place then rode up beside the other rancher. Dobie looked around; he was sweating. Jawn Henry said, "Who is he?"

Pierce answered softly as though he did not want to be overheard, but there was little chance of that. "Alls I know is that he come along right when I needed another man, an' he knows livestock. He never says much. My other two fellers sort of get along with him but they don't cotton to him. Neither do I, t'tell you the truth, Jawn Henry. One of my steady riders told me Horn Thompson drew an' shot a coiled rattler off a flat rock quicker'n the eye could see. They was ridin' through brush. The rider — his name is Redd — he says Thompson never said a word. Just blew that snake's head off from a hunnert feet, holstered his gun an' rode on like nothin' had happened."

Jawn Henry gazed ahead where the dark-eyed man was beginning to pick his way because the brush was thick. Jawn Henry had been judging men all his life. Thompson sat a saddle like he'd been born to it. His thoughts were scattered by a flurry of gunfire out where the dust rose. There was a pause then another furious burst of gunfire. Jawn Henry thought that second fusilade had come from those dun-coloured buildings.

Leghorn Thompson drew rein and sat like stone looking above the manzanita limbs. To Jawn Henry he appeared to be sniffing the air like a hound dog.

When the others came up, Thompson addressed them without looking around. "Somebody's forted up among them buildings . . . Watch an' you'll see the fellers outside tryin' to get in close among the sheds for cover."

They watched. After the last exchange of bullets there was nothing moving for a long while, then, sure enough, a long-legged man sprinted, got behind an outbuilding, without having been shot at. The silence returned, shadows were beginning to form on the east side of trees, bushes and buildings.

Sam Nesbitt squinted skyward. The day was almost over, but a summertime sun would continue to hang up there for another few hours, but as far as Sam was concerned, he had not bargained for a damned war. There were too many men with guns down yonder.

Even by accident the chances of getting shot increased in direct ratio to the number of nervous men with loaded weapons. Sam wanted to see six murderers dead, but he was not a hot-blooded youth and hadn't been for about ten years. He did not want to be among the casualties.

Jawn Henry was calm, shrewd and unruffled. Brad Holifield seemed more like Leghorn Thompson, he too was unruffled and in no hurry, but he had the look of a fighting dog on a short leash.

When Thompson glanced over his shoulder he said, "We're goin' to run out of cover directly. I'm not real favourable of fightin' at night, but . . . " He shrugged and swung to the ground to hunker in front of his horse.

Brad also dismounted, but he remained standing with one rein dangling as he made a suggestion. "If for a fact, those are possemen from town, I could ride down, act like I heard the shootin' an' was curious."

Jawn Henry looked at Holifield; something in the back of his mind stirred. He and Brad had ridden together for quite a few years. He had seen Brad's reaction to a lot of situations but this was the first time they had been together anywhere near a gunfight. Brad was steady and unworried as he had been in other

142

situations, but this time his calmness was cold and calculating.

Jawn Henry sighed. He visualised Brad killing that man years back for which the wanted dodger had been printed.

Dobie was sweating like a stud horse beside his animal. He was a shrewd trader, a successful stockman, he liked whiling away an afternoon at Carney Witherspoon's watering hole in town, he liked a lot of things, but this was something he did not like. He hadn't had the kind of coordination required to be handy with guns since he'd weighed only a hundred and thirty pounds, and that had been close to fifteen years back. He now weighed well over two hundred pounds and was as grey as a badger.

Horn Thompson was watching ahead when he responded to Brad Holifield's calm suggestion. "Would they know you?"

Brad's gaze dropped briefly to the other man's back. "If they're from

Templeton I'd guess I'd know just about all of them."

"An' what'll you say when they ask how come you're so far from home?"

Brad answered a little testily. "I'll ask them what *they're* doing this far from town."

Thompson unwound up to his full height and turned. "Want some company?"

Brad's reply was short. "No."

The dark man studied Holifield for a moment then almost smiled. "We'll go ahead to the end of cover an' wait for you."

Brad put an enquiring look on Jawn Henry, who said nothing, just made a slight forward nod of his head. He was about to recommend caution when the gunfire started up again and as its echoes were dying Sam Nesbitt spoke to Brad. "If it's them murderers forted up, fine. If it ain't we've wasted three hours setting back here."

Brad mounted his horse, turned back down off the topout, rode among the trees for a fair distance before breaking clear and setting his animal into an easy lope in the direction of the buildings ahead with dust around them.

Dobie sank to the ground, flung sweat off and groped for his cut plug. With that example, Sam Nesbitt hunkered, thumbed his hat back and rolled a smoke.

Jawn Henry squatted trailing one rein and did not move as he and the others watched Holifield cover half the distance in sunlight which was less dazzling than it had been but which was still abundantly bright.

Evidently others saw Holifield too because the men among those buildings began to crane around. Several stood up to gawk and the hawk-faced man growled under his breath about that.

A small band of thirsty cattle came into view southward where they stopped. Evidently the nearest water was among those dun-coloured buildings, but dust aside, the smell of burnt gunpowder was a powerful deterrent.

The cattle stood down there for a long time, until a brisk exchange of gunfire erupted, then they headed back the way they had come in a clumsy lope with their tails over their backs like scorpions.

Dobie asked if anyone had a canteen. No one replied because there were no canteens. Dobie eventually wandered off on foot. Maybe there was a creek or sump-spring back yonder a ways but Jawn Henry, for one would not have bet on it.

The silence was enduring as Brad got closer. It was possible that even the forted-up men were watching him. Jawn Henry wondered if they would attach significance to the fact that Holifield was coming from the same direction they had used a few days back. Most likely not but he held his breath a little as Brad got among the outbuildings and was lost to sight.

Dobie came back red as a beet and with his shirt stuck to his body. He sat on the ground without a word.

Leghorn Thompson broke the silence. "Can't see him but there's been no ruckus."

Sam Nesbitt spoke drily. "If they're from town, like he said, he most likely knows every one of them."

Thompson surprised the others when he asked if the marshal from Templeton might be down there. He clearly had not heard about his dead cousin knocking the slack out of the marshal. Dobie hadn't either so when Sam Nesbitt told them, Horn Thompson put his expressionless look on Sam and said, "When?"

"A week or such a matter before the storm, near as I know."

Jawn Henry nodded. That would have been his estimate too. Very faintly someone was shouting among the dun-coloured buildings and Dobie blew out a ragged breath. "Jawn Henry, you know that widow-lady who lives down there?"

"No. I haven't been this far east in years. There was a feller named

147

Shortgrass or somethin' like that lived down there last time I was — "

"Snodgrass," exclaimed Dobie. "He died four years back. His widder's been running the ranch since . . . You suppose them forted-up fellers got her hostage?"

Jawn Henry thought that was a strong possibility. "If they caught her inside, but what I'd give some fat cows to know is — are those fellers inside the ones we're after?"

Thompson was concentrating on the land far ahead when he replied to Jawn Henry. "If their tracks lead over there, it'll most likely be them." He paused before adding a little more. "Six of 'em? I'm goin' to cook someone's bare feet until they tell me who shot Carl an' his missus."

Sam and Jawn Henry exchanged blank looks. As sure as water wouldn't run uphill the hawk-faced man was not making idle talk.

Dobie forgot his thirst and excitedly pointed. "Rider coming."

148

He was correct. The rider was loping over the same trail Brad had made earlier. There was no sure way to verify it was indeed Holifield for a long time, but no one doubted it.

Leghorn Thompson stood up, hip-shot with a dangling rein and both thumbs hooked in his shellbelt. He was assuming it would indeed be Holifield and was looking past as he figured things.

It would not be sundown for another hour or so, with dusk and night to follow in another hour after.

# 9

## A Fresh Development.

THE loping rider was indeed Brad Holifield, but he rode into the timber a half mile southward before turning up-country to the rocky place where the men waited. As he dismounted Sam took the reins of his horse. Brad beat dust off before speaking. Every eye was on him. When he spoke he addressed Jawn Henry and Sam Nesbitt.

"It's them. Those fellers from town, an' hell even Tom Clancy, Carney Witherspoon, just about everyone who owns a gun's down there."

Jawn Henry was satisfied about the identity of the townsmen. "How come them to be up here?"

Brad brought forth his cut plug and held it away from his face until he had replied. "The lady who lives down there's got an In'ian ridin' for her. The outlaws come in last night just shy of sundown when the bronco was comin' back from his ridin' chores. He set out a ways watchin'. When he heard the woman holler he dusted it to town. It's quite a ride. By the time word got around with the fellers from Templeton ready to ride, it was late this mornin'."

The dark man had a question for Brad. "How'd the tomahawk know it was the outlaws who raided their town?"

"He didn't know it. Neither did the others. They figured it was one of them rovin' renegade bands."

"Did you tell 'em about the Mackensens?"

Brad considered the hawk-faced man for a moment before answering. "I told them nothin' except that Cloverleaf was shy some cattle and I was sent this far out while the other fellers looked in different directions."

"Did they say anythin' about you leavin' to come back here?"

"No; why should they? Everybody loses cattle now an' then. I wished 'em well and turned back. They got somethin' on their minds other than a rangeman hunting strays. I knew most of 'em, they had no reason to believe I lied to 'em."

Leghorn Thompson lost interest in Brad and turned back facing eastward. Sam nudged Jawn Henry. "How did they know who them renegades was?"

Brad heard and replied. "They had no idea. Like I already said, all the tomahawk saw was six men pushin' into the house an' he heard the woman scream. When the townsmen got up here and set up their surround, there was some palaver. One of the outlaws said they had friends comin' who'd get behind the townsmen an kill 'em ... This same feller said they'd all get what that damned banker got down in Templeton."

Sam Nesbitt was half-listening. He

152

was watching Leghorn Thompson. Something stuck in his mind. When Dobie had been asked how come he and his rider were this far east of their range, the question had not been answered to Nesbitt's satisfaction. He spoke aside to Jawn Henry, who scowled in thought for a moment, then put the question to Doughbelly Pierce.

The answer Jawn Henry got still did not satisfy Sam Nesbitt. Dobie said, "Horn said he thought he'd heard gunfire, so him an' me come over this way. I didn't hear no gunfire, but we rode easterly. After a dozen miles he just kept ridin' so I did too."

Sam Nesbitt got busy rolling a smoke. Jawn Henry was again distracted by a straggling exchange of gunfire down yonder.

Nesbitt lit up, caught Jawn Henry's eye and jerked his head. The fight down yonder was brisking up. No one missed two men who walked back a ways where Sam said, "Jawn Henry, how far would you say we was from the Pierce place?"

Jawn Henry guessed. "Maybe ten, twelve miles."

Sam's perpetually squinted eyes were fixed on his employer. "Did you ever hear gunfire that far off?"

Jawn Henry did not reply, he stared at his rider a moment before going back where the distant fight was trickling down until it halted altogether.

Sam resumed his former squatting position and also looked down where the dust was. He smoked and sat squinty-eyed and pensive. He did not once glance in Jawn Henry's direction or toward the hawk-faced man.

Brad was restless. Doughbelly wasn't, he was thirsty enough to drink green water. He also seemed perfectly willing to sit right where he was until the cows came home.

Leghorn Thompson considered the position of the dying sun, considered the open country ahead and when Brad said, "Be an hour before dusk," Thompson seemed not to have heard.

He was looking toward the sun-shadowed buildings again. "Yeah. The trouble with darkness is that in this kind of a mess it's as easy to kill a friend as an enemy, or to get yourself killed."

He gave none of them an opportunity to respond although in this kind of a situation there was no need to reply to the obvious.

Thompson led off riding easterly and a tad southward. He turned toward the others to speak again. But it was a while before he said a word. He looked at Sam and Jawn Henry, both were a tad shorter and heavier than he was. He considered Brad but only for a moment; Brad would never agree to what Thompson had in mind. He ended up gazing at Dobie, and although he seemed dissatisfied, he said, "Trade clothes with me, Dobie."

They all looked at the dark man as surprised as they were perplexed. Doughbelly stared at his hired man. "What did you say?"

"You been around here longer'n

most, haven't you?"

"Except for Jawn Henry I expect I have. Why?"

"Because those townsmen down there would know you by sight like they did Mister Holifield, an' I figure to ride down there like Mister Holifield done. The only way I can do that with dusk comin' since they don't know me but they do know you, is for me to dress in your clothes."

For a long time no one said a word. Brad was gazing steadily at the dark man. "If you wait to do somethin' like that until it's full dark, there wouldn't be no need for a disguise."

Thompson's black eyes swung to Holifield. "Partner, I don't like the idea of any of us ridin' down there after dark. You recollect what the forted-up feller said about friends comin' to flank the townsmen?"

Thompson did not elaborate. After another long silence Sam Nesbitt, still squatting, put his squinty gaze on the dark man. "An' what you got in mind once you get down there, Mister Thompson?"

The dark eyes changed position again. "You seen what's been goin' on down for a couple of hours or more. What townsmen did you ever see who had the guts to get right up to that house, maybe even get inside, and shoot them renegades?"

Sam did not reply. For a fact there was no reply. Men like the liveryman and the saloonman down yonder were novices at what they were trying to do. That darned fight could last for days, until the townsmen gave up and rode home, or the killers in the house ran out of ammunition.

Jawn Henry looked at Doughbelly as did Brad and Horn Thompson. Dobie squirmed. "There's got to be another way. Horn, you'd never look like me, even in poor light."

Thompson nodded and fingered the blanket under a saddle. "I can get enough padding, Dobie." He blew out a sharp breath and scowled at his employer. "Maybe you want to set here 'till kingdom come, but I don't an' I doubt these other fellers do. Dobie, this damned thing could drag on for a long time. Those renegades are forted up. If them town lads had a cannon — but they don't have, an' we all got somethin' better to do than growin' old settin' up here with no grub an' no water."

The last word Horn Thompson pronounced worked on Dobie like a physic. He struggled up to his feet, tossed his battered old hat and followed this with his shirt, which smelled and which hung on Horn Thompson like a tent.

They did not exchange britches because, as Sam Nesbitt remarked, it would be dusk by the time Horn Thompson got down where the townsmen could see him, and moreover one pair of soiled, greasy and faded britches looked about like every other pair.

Thompson was donning the shirt

and turned as though Nesbitt had not spoken to yank the blanket from beneath Dobie's saddle. The cowman looked pained about this but said nothing. No question about it, Doughbelly Pierce had a mountain of respect for his hired man.

When the dark man had made his saddleblanket-paunch the others considered the transformation with obvious skepticism but, as Thompson had said, with failing daylight the ruse might work.

It seemed just shy of insanity to Jawn Henry, but if Pierce's rider wanted to ride down there imitating old Dobie, it was all right with him. By now Jawn Henry and his riders had come to react toward Thompson like most men would have. They did not particularly like him.

Thompson did about as Brad had done, only he went so much farther south through the timber there seemed to be reason to believe he was never going to emerge at all.

But he did. His approach was from the southwest and he did not lope, he seemed to be pacing his arrival in the vicinity of the battleground to coincide with late dusk.

Nothing was said as the rangemen atop their rocky eminence watched the solitary rider heading toward those buildings which were now east of him and a fair distance north.

Brad Holifield sat on the ground. He did not look like someone who wished the hawk-faced man well. The others including Dobie, sat, mused and watched. Dobie had been unable to latch Thompson's shirt any farther down than the first two buttons, with the result that his distended gut showed a well-worn and none too immaculate undershirt stretched to its limit over something that could have been, but wasn't, a record breaking watermelon.

Sam Nesbitt chewed jerky from a saddle pocket. Brad and Jawn did the same but with less mastication as they put their full attention on

160

the distant rider. Jawn Henry made an observation.

"He should have taken that big horse of Dobie's. Even in poor light they'd recognise an animal that weighed twelve hundred pounds and belonged in harness not under saddle."

It was a good observation but no one commented. Leghorn Thompson was too far off now to be recalled, and Sam Nesbitt, at least, would not have called to the dark man to point out the mistake even if he could have. Sam was again entertaining some uncharitable thoughts that he kept to himself.

Dobie thought his tongue was getting thick, which it wasn't, but Pierce had been bad off with thirst other times and remembered what happened when a man's system had used up enough moisture to torment him for the moisture to be replenished. Along with the craving came tongue-swelling. A man had to be much farther along than Dobie was before this happened, but at the moment with shadows among the trees no one could have convinced Dobie of this.

He finally left the others, flopping-open shirt and perilously sagging britches. No one seemed to notice but of course they had noticed. Jawn Henry was also thirsty, but not *that* thirsty. Brad said Pierce's copious sweating, had dehydrated him without saying why that might be so.

Sam Nesbitt said nothing. He was watching Leghorn Thompson. Shortly before the hawk-face reached the thicker shadows down at those buildings, Sam rolled and lit a smoke and said something in a laconic tone that caught and held the attention of his remaining companions.

"Now why would a man in his right mind go to all that trouble to fool the townsmen down yonder? Hell, they most likely wouldn't shoot him if he commenced yelling who he was an' who he worked for an' repeated it until he was among them."

Brad and Jawn Henry looked at the

squinty-eyed man, waiting for more but Nesbitt did not add anything to what he had said, he enjoyed his smoke in silence. It seemed that Sam had expected to be questioned and when he wasn't, he said a little more.

"Ever since we come onto him'n Mister Pierce he's been more interested in what was goin' on down there than anythin' else . . . An' there's somethin' else: Jawn Henry you never heard gunfire from ten miles off, did you? Neither did anyone else. But he convinced Doughbelly of it an' led him over here — where he's been actin' like a cat on a hot tin roof."

Brad scowled. "Sam, spit it out, will you?"

Nesbitt smiled and was stubbing out his latest smoke when he replied. "He's gun-handy or I'm a Messican's uncle. He didn't hear no gunshots from Dobie's yard. He come over here for some other reason, and brought Dobie along for whatever he had in mind . . . You care to know what I think?" Sam allowed no time for an answer. "I think . . . you recollect that one of them forted-up bastards told you, Brad — someone was comin' up behind them lads from town?"

Brad and Jawn Henry stared at the narrow-eyed man for a moment before Jawn Henry said, "Sam, those fellers forted up down yonder killed his cousin."

Nesbitt remained unshaken. "That's what he said, for a fact." The ring of strong doubt was obvious in Nesbitt's response to Jawn Henry.

This new development kept the other two Cloverleaf men silent for a long while, until a faint shout came up to them in the failing light of day. It was clarion loud but the words were indistinguishable. Sam Nesbitt arose, dusted his britches and looked at Jawn Henry, who also arose. It was safe now to get down closer to those buildings.

As they picked their way through loose rocks Brad eyed Sam for a long while before speaking. "Naw; that feller who yelled from the house said *friends* was comin' not one friend. Not one friend."

Sam still remained unshaken. "What would you say if you was surrounded with no way out? You'd lie like a king an' so would I."

Jawn Henry, who had been silent since his rider had given his opinion was about to speak when all hell broke loose up ahead. The buildings were no more than uncertain squares but muzzleblasts were identifiable.

There was a short lull then it started up again. This time the first gunshots seemed to come from a somewhat localised place and the blossoming return-fire went mostly in that direction, but also went in other directions. Jawn Henry sat still trying to see something beside gun flashes. When the noise died out again he said, "Them first shots come from north of the buildings somewhere, like it was maybe two men or maybe even three."

Sam re-stated his suspicion. "One man could have done that, Jawn Henry, if he was nimble after each time he fired."

Brad said nothing as they rode onward at a slow walk. When they could make out the squareness of buildings Brad halted, rested both hands atop the saddlehorn and scowled. If Sam was right, if one man was making out he was more than one man, the little lulls were just about as long as it would take for him to shuck out spent casing, plug in fresh loads and start firing again.

As he, Jawn Henry and Sam sat listening and looking, the same pattern emerged again. A couple of shots, some answering ones, then four more shots and a regular fusilade, and this time the firing did not stop for as long as would be required for other men to reload.

Jawn Henry rubbed his scratchy jaw. He was dumbfounded at the idea that a renegade might have been among them all that afternoon. He did not have to re-assess the hawk-faced man, like his companions he had made his judgement of Leghorn Thompson. The dark man was anything but a greenhorn. The fact that he had waited almost until dusk to swap clothing with Dobie and go down there alone . . . Jawn Henry leaned to see around Brad to Sam. He said nothing, just re-appraised the man he had known for some years. As he straightened in the saddle a real fight broke out complete with red fire-flashes like fireflies, only now they did not appear to be as confined as they had been earlier.

Jawn Henry said, "Son of a bitch!" and squeezed his horse. As he led out Sam cautioned him. "If they see us . . . "

Jawn Henry heeded the unfinished warning, drew rein and sat with his companions, out of gun-range but well within sight of what seemed now to be a full-scale fight with muzzleblasts coming from all directions. As they watched someone yelled. The sound of desperation was audible in that voice as far out as where the Cloverleaf men sat. It was taken up by other shouts and later the sound of running horses.

Jawn Henry said it again, but with more emphasis this time. "*Son of a bitch!*"

Those running horses were breaking away southward, back in the direction of Templeton. The mob of townsmen were being routed because those forted up outlaws had got outside the house!

Brad shook his head, spat amber and resumed his upright position with both hands lying atop the saddle swells.

Jawn Henry signified acceptance of Sam's theory when he said, "They didn't just break out. When someone began firing into the mob from somewhere near the house, it gave those murderers a chance to leave the house."

Sam was vindicated. "Wonder who that could have been, Jawn Henry — with no one outside firin' into the town-riders from outside the house?"

Jawn Henry did not reply. But Brad said, "Well gents, by mornin' we'll be right back where we started only this time there'll be seven of them against the three of us."

They sat a long time listening to riders scattering like quail but all heading in the same direction, toward Templeton.

Jawn Henry eventually made a suggestion. "What's sauce for the damned goose is sauce for the gander. Seven to one is bad, but we got the same advantage they had. Dark night."

Sam leaned around to gaze in Jawn Henry's direction. He looked incredulous. "We're out-gunned an' they're as stirred up now as a nest of rattlers."

Jawn Henry was tired to the bone, his nerves were frazzled, he was thirsty and hungry. He did what he had never done before, he snapped at Sam. "If you want to go home go! I came over here for a darned good reason an' I'm not leavin' until either it or me, is finished!"

Sam said no more. He wanted to light a smoke but no one in their right mind would even think about lighting a lucifer in this situation.

When some degree of silence had returned, Jawn Henry kneed his horse ahead in a cautious walk. Brad and Sam rode with him.

Sam still thought the odds were too great, especially that now those six murderers had a genuine gunman with them. Sam liked the darkness in exactly the proportions that his companions did not like it.

Jawn Henry halted near a stand of sickly pines. They left their horses there. Sam and Brad took carbines as the three of them started walking. It was still a fair distance from where they left the horses to the yard. The ground favoured a stealthy hike, it was soft loam churned to three inches of pure dust.

When they were close enough to hear

well they detected the short, snarling sentences of men and the rub of leather. The outlaws were saddling to continue their flight.

Brad spoke softly. "We'll still be behind them. A hell of a lot closer, but all that means is that, come daylight they can see us plain as day."

Jawn Henry was listening for a particular voice. He only heard it when someone raised his voice in a gravelly way to say, "What about the woman? Hell of a waste to just leave her."

The next voice all three Cloverleaf men recognised. It was cryptic, hard as stone with the same testy tone they had heard atop the rocky place.

Brad softly said, "Sam; you was right."

Sam said nothing. Neither did Jawn Henry. A commotion erupted down through the darkness north of the clearly discernible main house. This sound was something the Cloverleaf men had heard many times. A horse was bucking for all it was worth.

Jawn Henry brushed the arms of his companions and started forward. For the time being it did not matter if they scuffed stones or otherwise made noise as they approached the yard from the west side of the main house. A bucking horse and a man trying to stay on top would hold the attention of anyone close enough to witness the fight.

# 10

## An Ally —
## A Bucking Horse

THE darkness was complete. If there was to be a moon it was still some time off as three wraiths blending with darkness reached the east side of the house, crept forward until they could peek around in the direction of the barn.

The battle at the corral was still in progress. Each time the bucking horse came down the earth reverberated, but evidently the man was still on top because whenever he had a chance, he turned the air blue.

Ordinarily Jawn Henry would not have taken the risk; this time he did. The outbuildings were not unusually far apart, but they seemed to be as Jawn Henry led the rush across to the first one.

173

The barn loomed massive and thick. The corrals were behind it, as was customary. Jawn Henry listened to his heart. It seemed to him to be making enough racket to be heard across the yard.

Brad nudged him and using his Winchester pointed toward the doorless big barn opening. They were almost opposite it. Jawn Henry breathed deeply, then scurried like a rabbit. Brad was directly to his rear with Sam Nesbitt bringing up the rear.

Sam was now committed. Like it or not he kept pace with the men up ahead, but whereas they never took their eyes off that barn doorway and the stygian darkness beyond, Sam ran with his head swivelling from side to side.

The horse stopped bucking. The men inside the barn had no way of knowing who had won the fight until that recognisable testy voice said, "Let it go. Rope one of them other horses."

Evidently the bucking-horse rider had finally been dumped in the dirt.

Jawn Henry went cautiously ahead until he was close enough to the big rear doorway, then he flattened inside for as long as was required for his companions to join him before he knelt and risked a peek around.

Four of them had their animals saddled. One man was dusting himself off with his hat, two of his companions were moving to rope another horse — and hope to hell the next one would be rideable.

Sam and Brad peeked out there too. It was dark. Even though a mingling of men and horses could be discerned, they could only temporarily be detected as one or the other.

Someone roped a horse. It sat back on its haunches, hind legs settled, front legs stiffly forward, the way savvy horses would do when they were old enough to know that the puny two-legged thing that had roped them, did not have the weight to make them come forward.

The roper, braced and straining,

swore. The other man with a lass rope did better. The animal he roped was also experienced. It came up on the rope, not exactly docile but certainly tractable.

There were two men who had to retrieve their ropes.

The second man had no trouble with his animal. He bridled it first and stood on the reins as he removed the rope.

The man who was holding a taut rope on the stubborn horse snarled for someone to go behind the horse and kick him until he quit balking.

Two men moved to obey when Leghorn Thompson snarled at them. "Leave it be! Open the gate, get mounted and ride. Them townsmen'll be back after they screw up their nerves. We got to be long gone an' far off."

The only outlaw who did not have a saddle on an animal looked over his shoulder, saw his companions moving to obey Horn Thompson, and squawked for help. He was ignored.

The dark man was right. They had wasted too much time. He led his fresh horse outside, turned it a couple of times, when it proved docile he toed in and swung up. His friends did the same, except that two of them mounted while still inside the corral, a poor thing to do with loose-stock milling in fright, but they, like Horn Thompson, were in a hurry.

Jawn Henry eased around and raised his sixgun. He did that as one of those freak dead-silences occurred. The noise carried. It also galvanised the outlaws. Jawn Henry had to leap backward as gun-thunder erupted.

Brad darted across to the opposite side of the opening, cocked his sixgun, held it at shoulder level looking for a target. The renegades were leaving in haste.

The man on foot in the corral swore fiercely at their backs, let go the rope to the squatting horse, snatched up his bridle where his saddle was up-ended, and went frantically among the milling, frightened loose-stock to catch another animal.

Brad had a target as three men raced past the barn opening. They were less than twenty feet as they spurred furiously. Brad tracked the hindmost renegade. The man threw up both arms and went down the near side of his horse. His spur caught in the cinch but it seemed not to matter. As the horse fled after the ridden animals, his rider bounced along like a broken doll.

Gunshots erupted as fleeing men twisted to fire in the direction of the barn, something which kept Jawn Henry and his two riders away from the doorway.

The abandoned rider in the corral with milling, frightened animals, also fired from the hip when he had an opening, and ran to the side of the corral to scale it.

When it was safe, with the sound of fleeing renegades growing faint, Jawn Henry ran to the front barn opening as Brad and Sam got belly-down to peek in the direction of the corral.

The abandoned renegade dropped to the ground and ran. Sam tried a shot with little hope of connecting, and missed, but the sound of a gun firing behind him almost gave the abandoned man wings.

By the time Jawn Henry was out front slipping along the barn-front, the outlaw had already reached an ugly but functional outbuilding, flattened against the rear wall and waited.

Sam and Brad stepped out of the barn looking for targets among the fleeing riders, but they had made good time in the darkness.

Brad leathered his sixgun, turned back, went up through to the yard and saw Jawn Henry, sixgun high, waiting for the abandoned man to try another rush.

Brad said, "There's no place for him to go — on foot."

Sam made a dry remark. "Except inside the main house."

That was a possibility but the

cornered outlaw would have to cross considerable open area first. Jawn Henry, Brad and Sam waited.

Jawn Henry barely more than raised his voice when he said, "Messican stand-off, cowboy, but dawn'll be along directly. We'll get you."

There was no response. Jawn Henry had not expected there to be. He considered dashing across the yard; if they could get over there, their field of vision would be more inconclusive, and for a fact that son of a bitch could not remain behind his shed forever. He could not even stay back there until dawn.

Sam was briefly thoughtful before he said, "I'll get back over alongside the house. Get inside if I can 'cause sure as hell he's got to take the widder-woman."

Jawn Henry nodded. After Sam had left to go down through the barn, emerge behind it and walk to the far northern end of the yard before risking a dash to the opposite side,

Brad offered to make a run for the shoeing-shed opposite in order to draw the outlaw's attention, which would give Jawn Henry enough time to get down the south side of the barn where he could see behind the outbuildings and, hopefully, find the outlaw.

Jawn Henry shook his head. The cornered man would be waiting for someone to show himself. That was all he could do for the moment, hope to wing one of the men who had been in the barn, and who he suspected were the men Leghorn Thompson had told them had been west of the yard watching the fight, all three of which were range men.

Jawn Henry agreed with Sam. The reason the outlaw had run south was because he wanted to reach the main house, and his reason for this would be to hold the widow-woman hostage.

They could not let the man reach the house.

Brad did not like a stand-off. He fidgeted until Jawn Henry said, "I'll make the run over yonder, you watch my back," and before Brad could protest, Jawn Henry ran.

A gunshot broke the silence, but it had not come from the shed behind which the abandoned renegade had been, it came from a broken window at the main house, and although it missed, it did not miss Jawn Henry by much, his lower legs were peppered with small bits of gravel.

He had not run in a long time. The distance was not great, but his lungs pumped like bellows as he threw himself toward a log wall and leaned there sucking air.

There was no second shot but an angry voice called from the main house. "Try it again. Show yourself just a little you son of a bitch!"

Jawn Henry stopped panting. He was shocked. The voice had belonged to a woman and although he had heard women swear before it never ceased to shock him.

She had mistaken Jawn Henry for

an outlaw. He would have corrected that mistake but if he did his slight advantage would be lost; the outlaw would hear him too.

Silence returned, deep and menacing. The outlaw now knew the woman inside the main house was also waiting and watching, and armed.

Short of sprouting wings his chances of remaining alive were down to nothing.

A small pebble landed close to Jawn Henry. For three seconds he did not breathe. Sam Nesbitt came out of the gloom. "Didn't want you to shoot me," he said, moved ahead and peered out into the yard. As he pulled back Jawn Henry said, "Stay over here. To reach the main house he's got to cross that open ground for a few yards. Nail him; don't let him get inside."

Sam nodded, waited until Jawn Henry was out of sight behind their building, then leaned his Winchester aside and vigorously scratched inside his shirt. He would have given a month's wages for a smoke, and something that had driven Dobie Pierce in search of water came now to plague him as well. It had been a long time since he'd had a drink, and while water was not his favourite libation, right now it out-ranked whatever came next.

Jawn Henry scouted from ground level with his chin in dust before making the rush to the next southward outbuilding. As before, when he got over there, his heart was loudly beating. It was not the dash, that had not been over more than maybe four or five yards, it was the knowledge that a man was waiting for a good target from across the yard.

Brad tired of waiting in front of the barn and slipped down the south side. He wanted just one shot at the cornered man and he did not care whether it was in front or from behind.

Jawn Henry estimated the distance between the last outbuilding and the main house. It was a good long fifteen yards over naked land. He slipped back, called softly to Sam and told him to wait two minutes then start shooting. This was another notion that Sam disapproved of. The moment he fired his advantage would be lost. But he began counting as Jawn Henry loped back where he had been, studied the northeast corner of the house. Someone, a woman no doubt, had planted geraniums along the front of the house. They weren't even knee-high. If she had planted grapes, or maybe a tree, but she hadn't, bless her soul!

Jawn Henry was not conscious of the chill as he waited. When Nesbitt finally fired two rounds, the first separated from the second by a five second lull, Jawn Henry broke clear and ran like a deer. By the time he reached the corner of the house he was sucking air again.

The ruse either had worked, because he was not shot at, or the outlaw was no longer on the west side of the yard, something which did not trouble Jawn Henry; even if he had managed to escape in darkness, he was still on foot.

It had been a day and night of surprises. Jawn Henry leaned on the house waiting for his heartbeat to slacken, and his breath stopped at the nearby sound of a gun being cocked.

He froze.

A rough voice said, "Step away from the house where I can see you an' shed that gun!"

Jawn Henry let go a rattling breath of relief and did not obey. He turned, saw the carbine barrel pointed at him on a slanting angle from a window, and saw the determined face above it. He had met her before, but it had been years ago. He said, "Mizz Snodgrass be careful with that gun. I'm Jawn Henry Thomas from southwesterly some distance."

The square-jawed, almost masculine face continued to regard Jawn Henry for some time, before the woman tipped up the gun, eased the hammer down and said, "What are you doin' over here, Mister Thomas?"

Her tone distinctly said she was both suspicious and wary. "Was you ridin' with that band of — ?"

"I got two riders in the yard. One of those outlaws got bucked off. He's tryin' to reach your house. If you'll let me in, we can be ready when he comes — if he don't get shot first."

The mannish face was expressionless for a long moment. "All right, Mister Thomas. Go around back. I'll let you in from back there."

Jawn Henry tried to move soundlessly. He did, too, right up until he turned the corner in back where someone had left rusting wolf traps hanging from a spike, at least a dozen of them. Jawn Henry bumped into them. They rattled and clanged together.

The masculine voice spoke from farther along. "You need glasses, Mister Thomas."

Jawn Henry reddened as he approached the woman. He had never known her very well, or her dead husband either, for that matter. Right now he did not like her.

She held the Winchester in one hand and the door in the other hand. Jawn Henry nodded woodenly as he preceded her inside, where it was even darker.

She stepped around him as she said, "They tore things up, broke furniture. You keep in my footsteps."

Jawn Henry obeyed. When they reached the parlour where cold air was entering through two broken front-wall windows, she stopped, turned, stepped close and squinted as though to reassure herself who Jawn Henry was.

He said, "They murdered some settlers. Me'n my riders been after them since. There are seven of them."

"Be six directly, when that one on foot gets killed." She stepped away from a broken window and tugged Jawn Henry after her. One side of her face was swollen. It was also slightly purple which was not discernible in darkness.

She sagged, leaning on the grounded Winchester. "Years back me'n my husband fought off In'ians. Last night was worse. They got inside." She paused, swore with feeling and looked at Jawn Henry. "Did you leave your wife alone, Mister Thomas, because if you did, I'll tell you not to do it again. I don't know what this world is coming to. Trash riding anywhere they like, robbing and killing decent folks."

The one-sided conversation was broken by a gunshot, followed after what seemed an interminable period of time by another gunshot, then the unmistakable sound of Brad Holifield's shout. "I got him — the son of a bitch!"

# 11

## Two Bafflements Resolved

**B**RAD'S successful hunt had been accomplished in a manner Jawn Henry never would have approved of. He had crossed open ground to get in front of the same structure the outlaw was behind. Then he had waited and when a whisper of sound came, Brad had stepped to the south corner in front, gun cocked and ready.

The outlaw was a tall, rawboned man, the kind who was fleet. He had to reach the main house and in order to accomplish this he had to dash from behind one outbuilding after another to get close enough for the final run.

Brad had stepped away from the shed in full sight. When the outlaw gave a lunging leap he too was exposed, but he was concentrating on the next

190

outbuilding. He did not even turn his head. Brad fired. Perhaps the only thing that saved the renegade from instant death was the changing spectrum. Darkness was fading, new-day light was spreading like a grey stain. This combination affected visibility even at fairly close range.

The bullet's impact broke the outlaw's stride. He was punched sideways and went down with a squawk.

Brad re-cocked his pistol and walked toward the man. He was gasping, pushing with one arm to get off the ground.

Brad leaned, hurled the man's sixgun and waited. He was coldly calm. The outlaw looked around. Dismal light showed coarse features, speckled beard-stubble and sunk-set eyes of indeterminate colour.

Brad said, "Get up!"

The outlaw tried, fell back and tried again. This time Brad caught him by the shoulder, and wrinkled his nose. If the outlaw had used soap lately it must have been some time before.

He steadied the man and called to the house.

Sam Nesbitt came warily across the yard, peeked around until he was reassured, then holstered his weapon as he approached Brad and the outlaw. He had no recollection of ever having seen the renegade before.

The wounded man breathed unevenly, the front of his shirt was torn and bloody. Brad swung him in the direction of the main house and called again. This time Jawn Henry answered as he opened the front door.

"Over here."

There were three wide steps leading to the front porch. Sam had to lend a hand before the outlaw could manage them. Jawn Henry held the door for them to pass through. In the centre of the room a sturdy, greying woman stood flat-footed without a shred of compassion showing.

As Sam and Brad lowered the outlaw to a chair the woman said, "Get a rag from the kitch. I won't have any no-good son of a bitch bleedin' on my furniture."

Sam found the kitchen, grabbed the first thing he saw, which was an apron, went back and told the outlaw to hold it over his front.

The hard-eyed widow-woman leaned, studied the outlaw for a moment, then went purposefully to her kitchen and returned with another cloth in her left hand and a whiskey bottle in the other hand. She snatched away the apron, flung the other cloth at the outlaw, handed Brad the bottle then stood back. "My Sunday apron," she lamented. "Blood sets up real quick." She left the men to put her bloody apron into a pan of water in the kitchen.

Jawn Henry told the man to drink, which he did, but there was no prompt reaction except when the wounded man moaned aloud. "Lef' me behind. Subbitches lef' me behind."

Jawn Henry lighted a lamp, put it

on a nearby table, pulled up a chair and sat down. "What's your name?" he asked.

The answer was slow coming. "John Jones."

Jawn Henry took back the bottle and leaned to tap the renegade's leg. "You can bleed to death for all I care, an we'll let you. One more time: What's your name."

The dirty, coarse-faced man looked steadily at Jawn Henry without speaking. Whoever he was, hatred ran deep in him.

Sam Nesbitt tried a different approach. "They left you knowin' you'd likely get killed. Maybe they'd be your friends but they sure as hell wouldn't be mine." Sam's effort appeared to meet with the identical lack of success as Jawn Henry's. The outlaw eased the cloth away from his wound and examined it by lamplight. If the slug had hit him just a couple more inches northward, as he had been running southward, he'd have been shot through the innards. As it was, the bullet had made a ragged incision from his left side to his right side without going any deeper than the flesh. It bled a lot and had seemed worse than it was. Lamplight showed that it was not the kind of injury the man would ordinarily die of. Unless infection set in, and there was reason to believe that would happen; the man was filthy, his clothing was dirty.

The square-jawed woman returned with sleeves pushed almost to her elbows. She stared at the renegade in good light and said, "This is the one that hit me."

By lamplight the swollen side of her face showed discolouration.

Brad smiled at the wounded man. "John Jones — name your friends."

The outlaw was still examining his injury. He neither spoke nor looked up.

Brad leaned, got a fistful of filthy shirt and with his face close, softly said, "Name — your — friends, or I'll break your neck."

The wounded man raised sunken eyes. "Only one I'll name for you," he said, "is the bastard who left me behind. I owe him for that . . . Horn Thompson. He can fry in hell. I'd help shovel the coal."

Brad released the man, straightened back and glanced at Jawn Henry, then at Sam Nesbitt. "You was right."

Sam shrugged. "Hell of a lot of good that'll do, they got fresh horses an' are most likely ten miles off by now."

The wounded man's venomous gaze went to Jawn Henry. "He come into the country a year or so back, got a ridin' job and studied out the town an' the countryside."

Jawn Henry asked the outlaw if he had known a man named Mackensen. The outlaw moved his eyes with a look of defiance to Jawn Henry. "I never knew him until Tex Carver led us to his place the night it rained hard."

Sam Nesbitt's eyes sprang wide open. "Travis Carver?"

"Yes. Him an' Horn Thompson

worked it all out. The rest of us thought it was crazy to turn north to that settler's place. Tex said they'd never figure we went north an' there wouldn't be no tracks for 'em to follow. It made sense, only we wanted to get out of the damned rain. He told us he knew a place where'd be safe an' dry. He never mentioned no grudge against that settler."

Jawn Henry began to faintly scowl. It was not to find a safe, dry place the former constable of Templeton had led the renegades to the Mackensen place, it had been to avenge himself on Mackensen for whipping Constable Travis in town, humiliating the lawman so badly that he had to leave the country. It was obvious now that the humbled lawman had planned revenge. Until the wounded outlaw named Travis, the Cloverleaf men'd had no idea who had led the outlaws. They now had a reason for the murders at the squatter's place. They also now had a name. Travis Carver, the former town constable of Templeton. Two names: Leghorn Thompson and Tex Carver.

Jawn Henry handed back the bottle, waited until the outlaw had swallowed several times then took it back and set it aside. They had the man talking. Jawn Henry's idea was that if the whiskey had helped before, it might help again.

Jawn Henry put his idea to a test. "Was it Horn Thompson or Carver who left you behind?"

"Both," growled the wounded man, who now had sweat on his face. He looked at the woman. "If you had some laudanum, ma'm?"

She did not move. "I'll give you a rope," she said.

The outlaw slumped. They carried him to a sofa. Before the woman would allow them to put him down she brought a blanket to put under him. As they eased the man down she leaned to say, "You better die. If you don't I'll wring your scruffy neck myself."

The Cloverleaf men exchanged looks.

Brad leaned to ask a question. "Where will they go from here?"

The outlaw rolled his eyes, shock had passed, pain had set in. His reply was husky. "As far an' as fast as they can." He looked at the woman again. "Lady, I'm sorry I slapped you, but if I hadn't they'd have shot you. When Horn asked where your cache was, he'd have shot you for not answering."

The woman did not appear appeased. She left the room.

Brad leaned and repeated his question. "Where will they go?" Brad placed powerful hands on the wounded man's throat, closing the fingers very slowly. "Where? I'd as soon strangle you as look at you."

The wounded man's eyes swung to Jawn Henry, who spoke softly. "Far as any of us are concerned, he can choke you to death."

Brad's grip tightened. The outlaw's eyes opened wide, he raised both hands to Brad's wrist. "To that cow outfit

Horn worked for. When he got inside last night and run off them possemen or whoever they was, he told us as soon as we chased them fellers clean away we'd head for the outfit where he worked. He said it was owned by a old 'possum-bellied feller who was scairt of his own shadow. We'd be safe there."

The woman returned with a blue bottle of laudanum. She spooned liquid into the wounded man's mouth and stepped back. He said, "Thank you, ma'm," and closed his eyes.

Jawn Henry asked about fresh saddle animals. The woman told him to help himself. She also told him among the corralled animals were two green-broke horses and two spoiled ones.

They left her with the wounded man as dawn arrived, visibility improved, and it was still cold.

They knew which were the spoiled horses, did not worry much about green-broke ones, roped three, rigged them out and left the yard as the sun half appeared above the eastern rims.

They were passing north of that rocky place where they had watched the fight the night before, when Sam Nesbitt wondered what had become of Doughbelly. Neither Jawn Henry nor Brad were sufficiently interested to reply.

They were encouraged when they cut the sign of horses heading in the same direction. The wounded man had either known in advance the route the renegades would take, or had made a good guess.

When heat eventually arrived they were close enough to Cloverleaf range to guess how much farther they had to go, and how much ground they had covered. As they slackened to a walk Sam Nesbitt said, "I ain't sure I'd want to be left alone with that woman if I was that feller."

Brad jettisoned a cud before speaking. "That ain't our worry. Me, I'd trade a good horse for a meal of eggs, bacon, coffee an' half an apple pie."

Sam wasn't worried about the outlaw

they'd left behind. He was trying to decide whether that steely-eyed, square-jawed woman would kill the outlaw, and while Sam was in favour of hanging the son of a bitch, he was a lot less sure women-folks should kill people.

The sun was high when they halted at a creek to tank up and give their borrowed animals a brief respite. They had been riding hard. Jawn Henry was of the opinion that if the outlaws hadn't gone to the Pierce place, had continued their flight northward, that he would have kept after them although neither he, his companions nor the horses they were riding were made of steel.

As they splashed across the creek, picked up the trail again, Brad fitted a fresh cud into his cheek and smiled for the first time in days as he offered Jawn Henry the plug of molasses cured. "Beats eatin' dust," he drily said. Jawn Henry smiled back. "Not if it makes a man as sick as a tanyard pup — which is what happened to me when I tried it."

Sam rode a while in thought before mentioning something else his companions had not considered lately. "Jawn Henry, it's goin' to be hard on them Mackensen children."

For about a mile Sam did not get an answer. He was beginning to think he never would get one when Jawn Henry spoke.

"Sam, Bess and I never had children." Jawn Henry paused; he would not have mentioned how hard they had tried if Nesbitt held a gun to his head. "Married folks should have 'em."

Nesbitt looped his reins to build a smoke as he asked the next, and obvious, question. "You figure to keep them?"

"That'll be up to Bess."

Brad put a black scowl in Nesbitt's direction and Sam, in the act of lighting up, did not say another word.

They did not have the Pierce place in sight until the sun was far down. They crossed another creek, offered the horses water, which they refused, and rode ahead until they could see the yard, which appeared empty. This was familiar ground. Jawn Henry led off into a bosque of standing pines. Brad was loosening the cinch to allow his borrowed horse more breathing space, when he thought he saw a rider southward and easterly. He leaned across his saddle-seat until he was sure, then spoke. "Yonder's Doughbelly."

Jawn Henry's brow furrowed. "He's comin' from the direction of our yard."

Nesbitt said what Jawn Henry did not want to hear. "Comin' from seein' your wife, I'd guess."

Jawn Henry swore under his breath. What Dobie had seen was not how things had turned out. Whatever he had told Bessie Thomas, would be bound to scare her.

Brad had the same thought. "Damned old potbelly scarin' folks."

They waited until Doughbelly was close then signalled him with their hats. He obligingly altered direction, rode into the trees wearing a look of surprise. "You three come through all right?"

Jawn Henry answered sarcastically. "No; we got killed. Was you at my place?"

"Yes. I figured your missus deserved to be told what was goin' on."

Jawn Henry was mad enough to chew nails and spit rust. His control was heroic. "Dobie, you didn't know what was goin' on. You went lookin' for water . . . Now you've went and scairt Bess. I ought to yank you off that horse an — "

Brad interrupted. "Dobie, them renegades are over at your yard. You remember that last lawman in town?"

"Tex Carver? Sure, what about him?"

"He's over there. He's one of them, along with your hired hand named Thompson."

Pierce sat his horse looking dumbfounded. "Leghorn . . . ?"

Jawn Henry replied. "Yes, Leghorn. We'll explain it to you another time. Right now we want to get into your yard an' you're goin' to help us do it."

The fat man said, "How? For Chris'sake Jawn Henry if they're over yonder," he gestured. "That's open grassland. They'd pick us off like crows on a fence."

"We'll wait until we can get over there without bein' seen," Jawn Henry said. "Get off your horse."

Dobie obeyed. He was still wearing the shirt he could not button more than two closures from his throat. He looked like the wrath of God, and from his expression he most likely felt it right now as he stared at Jawn Henry. "How do you figure to do that? Jawn Henry, let me tell you somethin', I'm a peaceful man who minds his own business and — "

"We've goin' to set here until dark, then you're goin' to lead the way, an' holler so's they know who is coming. Brad, Sam an' I'll be a short ways back. When they see you ridin' in, they'll — "

"They'll shoot me. Jawn Henry, for

Chris'sake you got to come up with somethin' better'n that. We could set out here until some fellers from town come out. Then we could — "

"No fellers from town are comin' out an' you know it," Jawn Henry exclaimed. "Now set down, get comfortable an' shut up."

Sam went as far forward as the first stand of trees. He watched the yard. Brad looked after the horses. They did not need a lot of care but Brad had not enjoyed the waiting for darkness last night and he did not like it now. But he approved of Jawn Henry's plan. Anything beat doing nothing.

He wasn't sure it would work, but last night he hadn't been any more sure and the three of them were still alive, gut-shrunk, filthy and tired enough to sleep standing up, but still alive.

Jawn Henry avoided Dobie, who did not complain — he knew that would be a waste of breath — and Jawn Henry was still angry about Dobie going down yonder and scaring hell out of his wife.

# 12

## Run To Earth

WITH the sun making its slow descent, gathering a rusty colour from cloud-dust as it sank, the men among the trees half a mile or so from the Pierce yard slept or fidgeted. Sam Nesbitt explained to Dobie what had happened back at that ranch where the battles had been fought.

Dobie listened open-mouthed, he still had trouble believing how deeply his hired rider was involved, although later he would not only believe Leghorn Thompson was up to his gills in the escapade, he would wonder what it was about Thompson that made Doughbelly fearful of the man.

Time always passed slowly when people were waiting. Brad and Jawn

Henry slept. Sam did too but not until Brad roused up so Nesbitt could rest. At no time did they leave Doughbelly alone. None of them were sure he would ride to his yard if he could, not after what he had been told about the men over there, but it was impossible to predict much about people.

Dusk settled slowly, very gradually limiting visibility. When Brad roused Jawn Henry they were of the opinion that if they rode slowly enough to keep pace with the descent of nightfall, it would put them closer to Dobie's yard than if they waited to leave the pines until full darkness.

Dobie listened to their talk and winced inwardly. He would not have wagered a plugged penny he would not get shot no matter how loud he yelled as he rode to the yard. When Jawn Henry brought his horse in to be rigged out, Dobie appealed to him.

"You don't need me out front hollering. As dark as it'll be directly you'll be able to get into the yard without me."

Jawn Henry put a look of distaste on his neighbour. "Maybe. But I like the notion of you bein' out front. Get your horse, Dobie."

"Jawn Henry, for Chris'sake — "

"Shut up and get the horse. *Now!*"

Dobie got heavily to his feet and went after his animal. During his absence the Cloverleaf men palavered. They still intended to put Pierce out in front, and they still agreed to follow him, but now they thought it might be better if only one of them shagged Dobie while the other two fanned out north and south because, if there was a fight, men apart from one another would be less liable to be hit than if they rode behind Doughbelly all in a bunch.

When they emerged from the trees it was possible to see a light ahead among the buildings, without being able to make out the buildings, which did not particularly matter, every one of them had been in that yard up ahead a number of times over the years.

Doughbelly whined about something Jawn Henry had already considered. "If it's them, sure as hell they'll have a man standin' watch. It's quiet enough for him to hear more'n one horse coming."

No one responded, but another dozen yards onward Sam angled northward while Brad did the same southward.

Dobie twisted in the saddle, saw only Jawn Henry behind, and sat forward with a loud groan. But he still said nothing, which pleased Jawn Henry. It would be a long time before Jawn Henry would forgive Doughbelly for scaring his wife out of her wits.

A dog barked. Jawn Henry stood in his stirrups, a waste of time in darkness, it was not possible to see the yard ahead. As he sat down the dog stopped barking, but only briefly. When he continued his racket, this time his voice was pitched lower, the way a dog would do when it had support from a man.

Dobie stopped his horse. Jawn Henry growled for him to ride on. Doughbelly did not budge. Jawn Henry rode up abreast of him and leaned from the saddle.

Dobie's face was noticeably paler than it had been, he had his right hand resting on the swells as he spoke without looking at Jawn Henry. "It ain't worth gettin' killed over."

Jawn Henry thought differently but sat in silence. The dog had stopped barking. Without a doubt it had roused anyone in the yard who might have been sleeping, or maybe just resting. He asked Dobie if he still had two hired riders. Doughbelly inclined his head without speaking. He wasn't sulking, he just was not going to talk. They were close enough to smell wood smoke, and that was too close to be healthy in Dobie's opinion.

Jawn Henry guessed the outlaws had neutralised Dobie's two hired men.

He was right but it would be a while before he would see his guess vindicated and meanwhile Dobie began another argument.

"Jawn Henry, you're being a damned fool. You'n your two riders. How many renegades are up yonder? Five, six maybe? Now that's no odds for a man with a lick of sense."

Jawn Henry reached, slapped Dough-belly's horse and kept it moving while its rider bitterly complained right up to the time the dog resumed barking, only more excitedly now.

Jawn Henry drew rein. Dobie did the same, with greater alacrity. The smoke scent was stronger. The outlaws had evidently made a meal.

Jawn Henry reined in close and tapped Dobie on the chest. "Yell. Tell them who you are an' that you're comin' in."

Dobie dug in his heels again, looked at his companion and said, "Shoot me right here because sure as hell they'll do it if you don't."

Jawn Henry's answer was quietly given. "You got a better chance with them than you have me. From this distance I couldn't miss with my eyes closed. In the dark they might miss."

Dobie stared at Jawn Henry. "An' we been good neighbours all them years."

"Call to them, Dobie."

The man with the expanse of gut showing where he could not button the shirt, sat a moment looking ahead before he yelled. "Arch, Dan, it's me, Dobie, shut up that damned dog I'm comin' in."

Jawn Henry leaned to lightly slap Dobie's horse on the rump. The animal started walking. Dobie twisted as far as he could and said, "It'll be on your conscience."

Jawn Henry waited until Dobie was difficult to make out before following. He looked left and right for Sam and Brad. There was no sign of them.

Someone hailed Dobie. Jawn Henry did not recognise the voice. "Pierce? You alone?"

Doughbelly lied with a clear conscience. "I'm alone. Is that you, Dan?"

There was no answer which confirmed what Doughbelly already knew. That voice had not belonged to either of his riders.

He rode slowly, entered the yard from the north with Jawn Henry a barely visible moving phantom farther back.

Jawn Henry dismounted and stood close to the head of his horse to prevent nickering as he watched not one man, but two men, approach Doughbelly from either side. They were armed with carbines. They came up as Doughbelly was dismounting at the tie-rack in front of his barn.

Jawn Henry could not hear what was said until Dobie raised his voice in indignation. "What you done with Chet an' Dan?" Whatever the answer was did not appear to ameliorate Dobie's indignation. He spoke again in loud indignation. Jawn Henry smiled. The old born and bred coward had found some courage after all. He was deliberately sounding angrily loud as he spoke again.

"Who? You're lyin, mister. Horn Thompson wouldn't do anythin' — "

The sound of a slap reached Jawn Henry. Evidently one of those men in front of the barn did not like being called a liar.

Another man spoke. Jawn Henry knew that voice, and wished Sam and Brad were with him. " . . . Why'd you think I traded shirts with you, old man?" Dobie muttered something before Leghorn Thompson spoke again. "Yeah? What'd you do, slip away from the others so's you wouldn't have to fight? Where are they?"

Whatever Dobie said, or did not say, got a savage response from Horn Thompson. This time Jawn Henry not only heard the blow land, but also heard Dobie's heavy body strike the ground.

Jawn Henry drew his belt-gun. He wanted just one shot at Leghorn

Thompson. He had to get closer, the range of a sixgun was limited. With a carbine he could have shot Thompson. Sam and Brad had carbines.

Jawn Henry moved carefully. When he could see them clearly, after the first shot they would be able to see him just as well.

Someone from the main house sang out. Jawn Henry used this distraction to move ahead nearly twenty feet, close enough to see Doughbelly sprawled at the feet of the three renegades.

Jawn Henry dropped flat. He could blend with the ground, standing up this close to the tie-rack, he would make an excellent target.

He did not listen to the man calling from the porch, his entire concentration was on Leghorn Thompson, who was twisted half around, not the best target but a good enough one. He raised up without haste, propped his right arm, steadied the gunhand with his other hand, cocked the weapon and fired.

Leghorn Thompson was punched

forward with arms flapping. The man on the porch bawled in surprise. Other men boiled out of the house. There was considerable blind shooting, none of it very close but Jawn Henry crab-crawled as swiftly as he could.

From the two sides of the yard Brad and Sam fired. A man in the act of leaving the porch was spun on the first step. He went sideways and rolled to the lower step.

The other men stampeded to get back inside. Dobie was scrabbling at dust as consciousness returned. Jawn Henry held his breath. Dobie was the only visible moving thing.

Brad and Sam fired into the house, which bought Dobie sufficient time to crawl past the doorless wide opening of his barn and to collapse in there where it was very dark and he no longer presented a target.

The fight brisked up. When Jawn Henry went back to lead his horse behind a building where it would be safe, Brad and Sam forced the battle, moving constantly as they did so.

Jawn Henry slipped behind sheds to the barn, went up through, glanced briefly at Dobie, who was lying still and sucking air, and inched toward the doorless wide opening.

The firing stopped. There were no echoes. Brad shouted. "Jawn Henry, have them other fellers go round behind the main house."

Jawn Henry did not answer. There were no 'other fellers.'

He put his hat aside, got belly-down and risked a peek in the direction of the main house. It was dark. There was no help from overhead where stars shone but no moon.

He methodically reloaded his hand-gun. Leghorn Thompson was lying out front legs wide and arms wide, face down. The renegade someone had shot off the steps was dangling half on, half off, the lowest step. Jawn Henry snapped the gate closed over his reloaded sixgun cylinder and liked the odds. There would still be five renegades in the house but at least this time they would not ride away.

He called back to Brad. "It's surrounded. The fire ought to start any minute."

Doughbelly yelped and struggled up to his feet. He ignored Jawn Henry to yell to whoever was out there. "For Chris'sake don't fire the house. You want 'em out of there — there's a box of stump-blowin' dynamite in the well-house."

Jawn Henry gazed at the fat man with a forming frown. Dynamite thrown into the house would cause as much damage as a fire. More, because aside from the explosion, a fire would follow the explosion.

For as long as was required for Jawn Henry to listen to the badly upset fat man, the yard was silent. Even the dog was quiet — for an excellent reason, after the first gunshot he had nipped under the house and was still under there shaking like an *hombre* passing a peach seed.

Very abruptly a man called from the house. Jawn Henry was not sure but thought he might be Templeton's former marshal. "You fellers give us horses an' we'll leave."

Someone laughed. It was a grating sound. Jawn Henry recognised the voice as the amused individual, Sam Nesbitt, called back. "That's exactly what you ain't goin' to do."

After another period of silence the same man tried again. "Who are you?"

Sam's reply was harsh. "It don't matter who we are. You're out-gunned five to one an' two fellers went after that dynamite."

Doughbelly clutched Jawn Henry's arm. "Don't let 'em do it. They'll blow my house to match sticks."

"Hell, Dobie, it was your idea, an' let go my arm."

A fresh voice sounded off. Dobie said, "That's Redd from the bunkhouse."

Jawn Henry had no way of knowing whose voice it was, but for a fact the yell had come from the log bunkhouse when a man said, "We told you sons of bitches . . . You're a goner." As though to emphasise his words the man in the bunkhouse, and another man in there, fired off three rapid Winchester shots. Evidently the firing had been without aim because Jawn Henry and Dobie Pierce heard lead strike solid wood near the westernmost front wall of the porch.

Brad and Sam opened up again. Jawn Henry, with no cover if he exposed himself, shoved his gunhand around and fired blindly. Again, the men in the bunkhouse joined in. For the first time it really did sound as though there were a number of men around the yard.

When the firing dwindled while men re-loaded, that same voice Jawn Henry had thought belonged to the former lawman of Templeton called out.

"We got money. Lots of it. If one of you'll come to the porch we'll hand it over — an' leave by the back door — providin' we got your word you'll let us get our horses and clear out."

Jawn Henry made a harsh laugh. "Mister, if all we wanted was your money, all we got to do to get it is blow you up with the house, then search the ruin."

"What the hell *do* you want?"

No one replied. Jawn Henry took a risk, stepped around the door opening, fired directly through a broken window and jumped back before return gunfire came from the house.

The sky was brightening a little. It was cold, stars were receding, hungry horses in a corral out back were milling and nickering. Doughbelly would not feed them; he would not leave Jawn Henry's side. Sure as hell they were going to blow up the house he had worked himself to a frazzle to build thirty years back.

He wanted to yell, to swear at the men taking his dynamite, instead he stood sweating hard despite the chill, his guts in turmoil, his swelling jaw where Horn Thompson had struck him, completely forgotten.

Brad yelled to Jawn Henry. "They got the dynamite out back. You fellers get behind something. They're goin' to use three sticks."

Doughbelly seized Jawn Henry's arm again. One stick of dynamite inside a house would wreck it, three sticks would blow the house sky high along with everything in it.

Jawn Henry pondered. There weren't any other attackers except himself, Brad, Sam, and those men bottled up in the bunkhouse. He leaned, made out the front of the house in watery dawnlight, stepped full forward balancing for a backward jump. No one shot at him.

He went back into the barn, went to the rear corral, opened the gate to free the loose-stock, then started toward the main house ducking from shelter to shelter. His hunch was that the renegades about to be blown up, were ranged along the rear of the house to locate and kill anyone back there with dynamite sticks. It was nothing anyone but a determined, or foolish, man would attempt; Jawn Henry wanted to reach the porch.

He was close to a smoke-house when someone yelled from the house. His voice bordered on panic. "Listen out there — we're comin' out. Hands high with no weapons. You hear me?"

No one answered for a long time, not until another agitated man yelled. "We give in. We'll come out, no use in usin' dynamite . . . All we ask is that you understand that we'll leave the guns behind, an' you won't shoot."

Jawn Henry called back. "Promising you nothing. Come out or get blown to hell along with the house. *Right damned now!*"

Time passed, the sky continued to brighten, the cold remained, those hungry horses which had been turned loose made a dwindling sound as they spread out in their rush to freedom.

Jawn Henry was about to call out when someone opened a heavy door, a man appeared fleetingly. He disappeared but the door remained open. Another man did the same thing, stood briefly in the doorway clearly visible, then got clear.

Brad yelled in scorn. "What're you waitin' for? No one's goin' to shoot you. Walk out of there."

One man appeared in the doorway, went as far as the porch steps, glanced at the cooling body half on, half off the lowest step, braced and resumed walking.

They all came out. Jawn Henry was not deluded by that promise to leave weapons behind. When the last renegade was in the yard, he stepped into sight, sixgun cocked and held belt-buckle high as he and the haggard renegade exchanged stares.

Brad came from the southeast side, behind the renegades and Sam went over to kick open the bunkhouse door where the two riders had gnawed through their bindings. They emerged as Sam also walked up behind the renegades. One of the cowboys had an eye swollen nearly closed. By feeble morning light both the swelling and its discolouration were discernible. This man walked without haste up behind a long-haired, burly built renegade, tapped the man's shoulder and when he turned, the cowboy slashed him viciously across the face with a pistol barrel. The outlaw staggered with both hands to his face where blood seeped through.

Doughbelly stood looking down at the corpse of Leghorn Thompson. He did not move until Jawn Henry eased down the dog of his Colt and holstered it as he said, "Carver — you murdered two decent people."

The rawboned, hard-eyed former lawman said nothing. Brad and Sam searched the renegades, found two derringers and three boot-knives.

The sun exploded up over the eastern world, brilliance filled the yard but no heat, not yet.

# 13

## The Way Things Were

JAWN HENRY told Doughbelly to go to the house and rassle some breakfast. Doughbelly shuffled away, shied wide of the dead man on the steps and entered his house as warily as a man entering a den of snakes.

Jawn Henry had the prisoners drag the dead men into the barn; summer heat on bodies that had been shot made carcasses swell fast.

The outlaw with the torn face sat on the ground still holding both hands over his face. They left him there, herded the others over to the shoeing shed, and sat them down.

Jawn Henry and Brad walked back to the centre of the yard. Sam Nesbitt left the pair of Pierce-riders watching the prisoners. Both of those men were venomous enough to shoot at the slightest provocation. The renegades knew it and did not so much as shiver although it was still cold in the yard.

As Sam approached Jawn Henry and Brad, they had discussed what came next, were in complete accord, and told Nesbitt. Sam, who nodded slowly, turned and gazed in the direction of the smithy, which had three sides and a roof but no front opening. "It ain't like there's just one man," he said, turning back. Jawn Henry and Brad ignored that statement and also looked over where the men sitting on the ground looked back.

Sam went over where that injured outlaw was rocking a little. His hands and shirt were bloody. Sam hoisted him to his feet, led off in the direction of the trough out back, and released the man's arm as he said, "Stick your face in the water. It'll be cold enough."

The outlaw, a nondescript individual, ducked his head. The water turned pink. Sam pulled him around and pursed his lips in a soundless whistle. The man's nose was broken, the skin around his eyes was swelling. He had a gash angling across from his left cheek to the right cheek. That Pierce-rider had done a good job of spoiling the outlaw's face. He would wear a livid scar for the rest of his life . . . Maybe.

Sam told him to duck his head again, which the man did. Cold water not only rinsed the blood off, it also congealed the other blood and exposed the gash.

Sam said, "Feel a little better, do you?"

The man nodded. He no longer held his hands up, but when he breathed it sounded like someone blowing through a reed.

Sam asked the man his name. The outlaw answered without hesitation. "Brutus Monahan."

Sam's brow puckered. "What kind of a name is that?"

"Eyetalian. My paw read a lot of books. He named me after some feller who lived hunnerts of years ago."

"Brutus, who killed them settlers?"

"Tex Carver. We caught the feller in a spud patch. He was afoot, we was ahorseback. Tex got between him'n the house. It was dark an' sort of rainy. Tex waited until the clod-hopper was close, then shot him. The feller staggered into the house before he fell. There was a woman in there. When the rest of us come up, she was screamin' an' hollerin' over the body of the man . . . Makin' a hell of a racket."

"So Carver shot her?"

"No. The feller over yonder wearin' the butternut shirt — he shot her. She stumbled over to the bed and fell."

"What's the name of the feller with the blue shirt?"

"Orcutt. Doug Orcutt."

Sam considered his prisoner. "You ever seen a hanging, Brutus?"

The injured man stared. "No."

Sam jerked his head for Brutus Monahan to precede him. They walked around into the yard and Brutus stopped in his tracks.

Jawn Henry and Brad had gotten lass ropes from saddles and two of them were already dangling over the massive baulk in the barn's front doorway. Sam nudged Monahan, herded him to the shoeing shed where his companions sat and pushed him to the ground.

The cowboy who had struck Monahan, eyed the injured man with a pitiless stare.

Sam looked for the man wearing the butternut shirt and spoke to him. "Is your name Orcutt?"

The haggard, dirty renegade looked at Sam, at Monahan, and nodded.

"Why'd you shoot the woman, Orcutt?"

" . . . Her gawdamned screamin' got on my nerves." Sam nodded. "Yeah, I guess it would."

He walked over to the barn where Brad and Jawn Henry had the ropes in place. "You fellers know how to tie a hangman's knot?" he asked. Neither Jawn Henry or Brad responded. Sam was still looking up at the ropes when he said, "Neither do I, an' I guess it don't make any difference."

One of the renegades began rocking a little from side to side making little animal sounds. No one heeded him.

Doughbelly came out to the porch to say breakfast was ready, saw the ropes, and his throat closed.

Tex Travis called to the man in the barn doorway. "The law'll get you for this."

Jawn Henry answered. "What law? You was the law. You're also a murderer an' an underhanded son of a bitch."

Sam added his two bits worth. "A horsethief, a bank robber an' an all around bastard. There ain't no law, not after you'n that other marshal got run off . . . All we got left is natural law, which has always been the best kind to me."

Brad saw Doughbelly and called to him. "Breakfast ready?"

Pierce could not speak. He bobbed

his head like an apple on a string, groped behind himself for a chair and sank down.

They ignored him. The rangemen guarding the prisoners were not young men, but seasoned, hard as iron with the knowledge of what was coming and believed wholeheartedly in it, especially the one who had been struck in the face.

Jawn Henry had a question. "Carver, did Leghorn Thompson see you kill his cousin an' the woman?"

Carver sneered. "That damned sodbuster wasn't no more his cousin than I was. Did he tell you that? Leghorn would lie to suit anythin' he had in mind. If he told you that it was most likely because he wanted you to figure he was after us like you was. I'll tell you one thing. Horn Thompson was a sly son of a bitch."

"Was he there when you killed the settlers?"

"Naw. He was in the yard here."

"How did he know you'd be over at

that widow-woman's ranch?"

"Because he'd scouted the country an' told us where that ranch was an' that there was a widow-woman lived there, who had an In'ian for a rider. That was where he'd meet us."

Jawn Henry said, "But you didn't go there, you went to the settler's place first."

Travis Carver stopped talking. His stare was defiant as he settled his back against a large fir round with an anvil atop it.

Brad squinted at the position of the sun, it was high enough, there was warmth in the morning. He looked at Jawn Henry. "We could be home for a decent meal."

Jawn Henry nodded, told the cowboys to haul the prisoners over two at a time. They started with the pair of renegades nearest the forge. Both outlaws stood up, frozen-faced, haggard and filthy. They were herded by one rangeman over to the baulk where ropes dangled. Not a word was said, the yard was hushed, there weren't any birds in the trees.

Sam stood aside as the renegades were positioned beneath the ropes. Brad and Jawn Henry got their horses, rode through from out back and took the tag ends of two ropes, made their dallies and picked up the slack. At the very last moment one of the outlaws cried out a woman's name. The other man slumped forward in a dead faint.

Jawn Henry and Brad exchanged a glance before easing the horses ahead. They had neglected to tie the arms and legs, so that as the strangling men rose off the ground they flailed and kicked.

Jawn Henry and Brad were half the distance of the runway when they halted and looked back. Death came swiftly but the gyrations continued for a minute or two before Sam signalled for slack.

He removed the ropes, dragged the corpses aside and called for the next pair. This time one of the renegades, with nothing to lose, tried to run for it. Brad overtook him before he got far, knocked him down with his horse and as the dazed renegade arose, Brad cocked his aimed sixgun. If the outlaw hadn't been dazed he might have chosen that way to die, but before his mind cleared a Pierce-rider and Sam Nesbitt had him between them.

The second pair of outlaws had sweaty shirtfronts and it was not that warm yet. One of them asked for a drink of whiskey. To get a bottle took time. Sam got it and the outlaw threw back his head, drank deeply and nodded to Sam as he handed back the bottle.

This time Sam used pigging strings to bind their arms and ankles. He believed in the hangings, he just did not like watching men struggle wildly against being strangled.

They saved Tex Carver to the last, let him sit over there watching each of his companions die a relatively slow death.

When Doughbelly's riders prodded

Carver to his feet he screamed and lunged at the nearest man. Both riders clubbed the fight out of him, let him lie briefly before hoisting him to this feet and while gripping him on both sides led him across where only one lariat still dangled.

He shook the man off, turned, positioned himself beneath the rope and swore at the men around him. Sam had to lash his ankles while one rider gripped him from behind to prevent Carver from kicking.

As Sam straightened up, facing the former lawman from a distance of no more than three feet, Carver cursed him for fifteen seconds without once repeating himself.

Sam stood expressionless until the tirade ended, moved around to lash Carver's arms in back, then pulled the lass rope low enough to fit the slip-knot over the condemned man's head. In a dead calm voice Carver said, "Pull my collar up. That damned rope is scratchy."

Sam obliged, still wooden-faced, moved around to face the renegade and spoke quietly. "You're lucky. You're goin' out quick. Years back I saw a feller like you get tied behind a wild horse. We heard him screaming for almost a mile."

Carver's gaze at Sam Nesbitt was steady, unwinking. "You're goin' to be haunted by this all your damned life. I hope you never sleep, mister."

Sam stepped back and raised his arm. He and Travis Carver looked straight at one another until the horse picked up the slack, kept picking it up until Carver was about four feet off the ground, arching and straining, twisting, opening and closing his mouth, eyes wide and bulging.

Sam went out into sunshine with his back to the dying man and rolled a smoke with steady hands. The only sound as he lit up was made by the rope over the barn baulk and the jerking of the man at the end of it who was turning back and forth.

There was no sign of Doughbelly. He had fled into the house after the first hangings.

When Sam faced back around Jawn Henry was backing his mount to let the dead man down gently.

Sam went back, cast off the ropes, watched his employer and rangeboss ride out the back of the barn, returned to the sunshine to smoke and consider an unblemished expanse of blue sky.

The three of them got their animals, watered them out back, snugged up and stepped aboard. They nodded at the pair of Pierce-riders and left the yard around the west side of the main house. They did not see Doughbelly, and they did not speak for several hours, not until they had Cloverleaf rooftops in sight, then Jawn Henry said, "Less said the better."

Sam and Brad nodded.

"I expect it'll be talked about in time."

He was right about that.

"But us three don't have a thing to

say. Nothin' to nobody."

Sam and Brad nodded again. Brad lifted his hat, pushed sweat off and lowered the hat. It was a beautiful day, not too hot, the air was as clear as glass, larks were in the grass, distantly Cloverleaf cattle were getting as slick as moles, and Bessie was on the porch watching their approach. She was alone. Jawn Henry wondered about the children.

He waved, Bessie waved back, continued to lean on the overhang upright as they rode in, swung off and led their animals inside to be cared for.

Out back, the horses drank, turned a couple of times then went down and rolled, stirring manure-scented dust.

A large, muscular man appeared in the rear barn doorway. Brad smiled. "Good to see you, Chet."

Jawn Henry asked if he'd got hold of the medicine man. He had. "You said fetch him even if I had to use a gun."

Jawn Henry nodded. "Did you have to?"

"No, but he's a real stubborn man. I had to knock him senseless, dump him in the buggy an' he never come around until we was halfway back."

"How are the children?" Jawn Henry asked.

"Fine, I guess," the large younger man said. "The lad's all over the place, gets under a man's feet like a puppy. The girl . . . Well she's pretty sick. The doctor stayed with her for a spell and left behind enough medicine to cure half of Templeton . . . I took him back in the buggy. He wouldn't talk to me."

Jawn Henry nodded about that. Elias Farrar was not an individual who would take getting knocked unconscious and abducted as all in a day's work.

Jawn Henry left them at the barn. Bessie was still on the porch as he struck out across the yard.

# 14

## Some Changes

**B**ESSIE made supper while Jawn Henry went to a back bedroom where the little girl was lying small in a big bed. He sat down on the edge of the bed and smiled. She did not smile back. If Jawn Henry could have been himself he would have understood.

He took her hand in his. She didn't have good colour and her lips looked chapped. He told her he and his wife were real pleased to have the children with them. He also told her that her brother was having the time of his life.

She looked steadily at him. "Did you . . . bury them, Mister Thomas?"

Jawn Henry was caught cold. He glanced out the window. "Yes, we buried them." He looked back. "We'd be real proud if you'n your brother would stay with us."

The girl's face was frozen except for the eyes, they gradually filled with tears. She freed her hand, rolled over, clutched a pillow with sobs shaking the bed.

Jawn Henry stood up. He wanted to take her in his arms but instead he returned to the kitchen. Her brother was out there with Bessie. He too, did not smile when Jawn Henry held out a hand. The lad shook it and released it. Bessie said, "Honey, the wash basin's out back on the porch."

After the lad departed she looked at her husband. "You need a shave, Jawn Henry, an' an all-over bath. I'll help you fill the tub after supper."

He got the bottle from its hidden place, sat down, waited until Bess half filled the cup with hot java, then tipped in the bracer. She said Mister Pierce came by.

Jawn Henry nodded, sipped coffee

and settled against the chair. "The girl asked me we'd buried her folks . . . she busted out crying."

"It's been most likely the worst thing that'll ever happen to them. Fortunately they're young."

Jawn Henry emptied the cup and looked at his wife. "What did Dobie tell you?"

"Well . . . He said he got over there too late for the fight, but from where he was he could see it goin' on; the odds were against you'n the riders coming out alive."

Jawn Henry's face reddened. He refilled the cup and splashed in another tad of whiskey. He did not trust himself to speak, so he took the cup with him and went to shave and wash. Odd thing about folks; Dobie had been a good neighbour for a lot of years. Jawn Henry had always liked him. Maybe, because they lived miles apart and rarely visited, Jawn Henry had not really known Pierce. He sure as hell knew him now. He did not feel particular dislike, just disgust.

He returned to the kitchen, sat opposite the Mackensen boy and ate like a horse. Bessie tried some conversation but it did not take. Jawn Henry was starved and out of sorts.

The Irish coffee had not brightened his mood, it had done the opposite. The next time he and Dobie Pierce met on the range Jawn Henry promised himself he would blister the old devil from poll to hocks.

The lad's voice was still high, but occasionally it broke, sounding deeper. "Mister Thomas . . . ?"

"Yes, boy?"

"Missus Thomas said you'd do the Christian thing."

Jawn Henry straightened up, put down his knife and fork and gave Bessie a perplexed look. She said, "He means about his folks."

"Oh." Jawn Henry avoided the lad's gaze. He did not want another crying heart-broken child. He forced a smile and said, "Yes, son, we done the

Christian thing."

After supper Jawn Henry sat at the kitchen table until Bessie returned from bedding the child down. He said, "Didn't you tell him Brad an' me buried his folks?"

"Yes. He took it better'n his sister, but he ran out to the barn. I let him get all cried out before going after him. He's much better, but his sister — "

"Bessie, if he knew we buried his folks, why did he want to know if me'n Brad done the right thing?"

"He meant, did you say a Christian prayer over the graves. His folks asked blessings before eating, and had prayer meetings at their soddy every Sunday."

Jawn Henry continued to regard his wife. It was beginning to dawn on him that having two children was going to require changes, starting with praying every Sunday and maybe reading from The Book, things Jawn Henry did not object to, but things he had not done since he'd been the age of the Mackensen children.

Bessie leaned, kissed his forehead then got busy cleaning up the supper mess. He watched her, she had a strangely sweet expression on her face. Jawn Henry was not an authority on women, but he *was* an authority on one woman.

He bedded down early, did not awaken until close to high noon the following day, and entered the kitchen to find his wife and Axel Mackensen filling the bathing tub for him.

He ran them off, bathed, was not particularly surprised at the colour of the water, and was bailing it empty out the back door into Bess's geranium bed, when someone discreetly entered the kitchen while he was out back to place clean underwear, socks, britches and shirt on a chair.

It made a difference. Jawn Henry kissed his wife's cheek and mussed the lad's hair before eating breakfast. By the time he got down to the bunkhouse it was mid-afternoon. His riders had also bathed and dressed in clean attire.

They too had slept the clock around and half again.

As Jawn Henry reached for the latch to enter he heard Sam Nesbitt say, "Of course I'm not goin' to say anything. All I said was that old pus-gut Pierce will. I expect first he'll bury the bodies then he'll high-tail it for town, an you know he'll get free drinks for his story."

Jawn Henry pushed inside, nodded around and sank down at the bench which served as the seating place for anyone eating at the long, wide old scarred table. He looked first at Nesbitt, then at Brad and Chet. "It don't matter what Dobie says. *We* got nothin' to say. Folks in town can think what they like."

The youngest rider, muscular and large Chester Bolling had heard the details the previous night. "Folks know Mister Pierce is a windbag . . . Besides, that's the way things is done. Pure and simple."

"An' there isn't no law," Brad stated

as they heard riders enter the yard. They all stood up looking at Jawn Henry. He wagged a finger without speaking, opened the bunkhouse door and walked out into slanting afternoon sunlight.

Tom Clancy the liveryman, was dismounting at the tie-rack. He called a greeting. "Good evenin', Jawn Henry. We come out to ask your rider if he'd like the job as town marshal."

The liveryman's statement took the Cloverleaf men totally by surprise. Jawn Henry did not reply until all four men from Templeton were on the ground. "What rider?"

"That one," the liveryman replied, pointing in the direction of Chet Bolling, who looked downright speechless.

Clancy leaned on the tie-rack. The men with him included the general store's proprietor, Carney Witherspoon, and Elias Farrar standing beside his horse wearing a long Prince Albert coat and black britches to match. He alone among the townsmen appeared stern.

Jawn Henry turned toward Chet Bolling. "It's up to you, partner."

The large man faintly frowned. "I don't know anythin' about bein' a lawman."

Tom Clancy responded dryly. "Well, seems you're a man as knows what he goes after. We talked about it this morning at the council chambers over the fire house. If you want the job, you can have it, an' the backin' of the town along with it."

Jawn Henry regarded the four townsmen. At least two, maybe three of them, had been routed at the widow-woman's place night before last; it seemed questionable to him how much the support of the community would be worth if Chet had to face real trouble. But he remained silent.

Chet, never talkative, said he would like to ponder on it. The liveryman, evidently appointed as speaker for the townsmen turned, looped his reins and smiled disarmingly. "Take all the time you want. We'll just set out here an' wait."

Jawn Henry and Brad exchanged looks. Brad seemed about to laugh out loud, Jawn Henry simply wagged his head.

Doctor Farrar asked how the Mackensen children were. Jawn Henry told him he could see for himself, they were over at the main house. The tall, unsmiling man marched across the yard.

Sam Nesbitt sat on one of the two benches in front of the bunkhouse and methodically rolled and lighted a quirley.

Chet faced Jawn Henry, a mute question in his eyes. Jawn Henry said, "More money for less work than working cattle, Chet. There'd be folks around too . . . I don't know what it's worth havin' the townsmen back you in trouble. Seems to me couple of nights back about fifteen of 'em let half a dozen renegades rout them. But it's up to you."

Carney Witherspoon got red in the face. "Jawn Henry, they didn't rout us."

"What would you call it, Carey?"

"Well . . . we was all set to starve 'em out. We was fixin' to surround the house and wait them out. But some son of a bitch got past us an' let 'em out. We was scattered pretty thin . . . We wasn't routed, we just rode back a mile or so so's we could re-group."

Silence ensued. Jawn Henry and Brad were expressionless except for their eyes, they showed hard amusement. Brad asked the saloonman if any of them had seen Dobie Pierce.

They hadn't. Jawn Henry was struck with an idea. If Doughbelly went to town and told folks about the lynchings, they would sure as hell ask questions. There would be no way Doughbelly could answer them all — providing he told the truth — without making himself look bad.

Brad startled the townsmen. "Have any of you rode over to that settler's place? That settler who run off Tex Carver an' that other town marshal?"

They hadn't, so Brad told them about the murders. While he was speaking, and for moments afterwards for as long as was required for the townsmen to absorb Brad's story, it was deadly quiet until a horse coughed and broke wind at the same time, something so commonplace no one heeded it.

The storekeeper said, "They had children."

Jawn Henry jerked his head sideways in the direction of the main house. "My wife'n I got them. The girl is sick. Farrar's been takin' care of her. The lad's fine. He's around here — "

"Doc never said a word to any of us," the storekeeper exclaimed. Jawn Henry put a hard look on the man. "He don't talk a lot at any time, does he?"

Chet spoke. "Did he tell you about me comin' to town to fetch him back to look at the little girl?"

The storekeeper shook his head. "No.

All he said when we met this mornin' over the fire-house, was that he thought you'd make a good town marshal. Folks put store by what he says. That's how come us to be out here."

Sam Nesbitt ground his smoke underfoot as he arose from the bench. Without a word or a glance at the others, he walked to the barn and disappeared down inside. When he got out back near the stone trough, he leaned on the corral and laughed. It wasn't finished yet, and it had been the craziest damned mess he had ever heard of.

Jawn Henry invited the townsmen to the main house for coffee. When they stood like crows neither accepting nor declining, he turned and lightly rapped Chet on the back. "Take your time," he told the younger man, then added a little more. "If it don't work out, you'll have a job here."

Jawn Henry entered the bunkhouse and sat down. Whether his rider accepted the offered job or not meant very little. If Chet still had the job in town when it was time to drive cattle to rails-end, he could find another man.

He went to rattle the bunkhouse coffee pot. It was empty so he returned to the table and sat down again. There were intermittent sounds of men conversing outside. Jawn Henry thought of Doughbelly. Maybe not right away, but sure as hell someday someone was going to see the graves, or maybe see something else that would arouse curiosity; horses bearing the brands of the men who had raided Templeton in broad daylight . . . Whatever it would be, the lynching of those men in front of Pierce's barn would not remain a secret forever.

As for Doughbelly . . . After pondering on it for a while he would know for a fact that the minute he told what had happened, the Cloverleaf men would tell their side of it, which would make Doughbelly look bad, and *that* was something Doughbelly Pierce could not afford to have happen, if he figured to continue to live in the Templeton countryside.

But hell, there was no way that kind of a story would not eventually trickle around.

Jawn Henry heard someone laugh out front and went back out there. Doctor Farrar was pinning the marshal's badge on Chet. He wasn't very good at it. Chet flinched when the pin stuck him. Farrar withdrew it, looked up at the large man and said, "I never apologise for puncturing folks."

Carney and Tom Clancy took their horses out back to be watered. Sam Nesbitt was back there. He watched them remove the bridles and loop the reins and spoke softly. "Usually you fellers who live in towns let 'em drink with the bridles in their mouths, then wonder why they get a bellyache . . . Did Chet take the job?"

Clancy, a lifelong horsemen, was prepared to rebutt that first remark, but did not get the chance. Carney Witherspoon spoke first.

"Yes, he took the job . . . You think he'll make a good town marshal, Sam?"

Nesbitt nodded. "He's big enough to throw a saddle on, an' most other ways he can handle himself well enough. He's young, but that don't last forever, does it?"

The three of them walked back up through the barn to join the others. Jawn Henry and the medicine man were talking slightly apart. Chet and the storekeeper were also conversing. Carney cast a sidelong glance at the position of the sun. It was six miles to town. He wanted to be back there for the evening trade, which he would not be unless he left Cloverleaf's yard soon.

He called to the doctor, jerked his head toward the doctor's horse, then nodded at the liveryman and swung astride.

After the townsmen had departed Chet went up to Jawn Henry. "I don't like to leave Cloverleaf," he said.

258

Jawn Henry smiled. "Better wages, Chet, an' when it's cold you can set by the stove in town. Another thing . . . riders got to set a higher aim or they end up like the old busted down gaffers you see in every town. Poor as snakes, stove up, lots of fine memories but awful short on what a man needs later on . . . like I said, if you don't like it, come back."

Chet shoved out a large hand. "I'm beholden to you, Jawn Henry . . . Expect I'd better saddle up and ride over there."

Brad, Sam and Jawn Henry watched the big young man ride west in the direction of Templeton. Brad said, "Good thing he wasn't with us yesterday."

Jawn Henry hiked in the direction of the main house. Sam and Brad went back to the bunkhouse. The day was nearly done, there would be chores to do directly but for a while there was time to sit and think.

At the main house Jawn Henry told

his wife what had happened out yonder. She had been anxious when she had seen the riders enter the yard. She had not asked her husband what had happened yesterday. In fact she never would ask him, but after a few years she heard enough soft-said remarks to have a good idea.

Jawn Henry went to the little girl's room. Her brother was nearby on a chair. They had been talking. The moment he appeared they became silent.

Jawn Henry sat on the side of the bed. He looked very different from the haggard, unshaven and dirty man who had been at the bedside the day before, but the girl still did not smile. Her face was expressionless but at least this time there were no choked-back sobs or tears.

Jawn Henry had never been around children. Only occasionally and rarely even then, but for some inexplicable reason he felt at ease as he asked the girl if she felt better.

She nodded. "The doctor gave me some grease for my lips. He said when people had high fever their lips dried and cracked."

He knew exactly what was on their minds. He also knew he would not mention it in detail until he thought they were ready to hear it. He asked the boy if he liked horses, a fair question for boys his age wherever they were.

"My sister'n me rode a lot. We found an old In'ian camp once." The boy raised shy eyes. "You got a lot of horses, Mister Thomas?"

Jawn Henry nodded. "Quite a bunch. I don't exactly know how many . . . When your sister's ready, we can go find a couple for the pair of you."

The girl's eyes brightened. Jawn Henry saw this and pushed ahead. "Sometimes me'n the riders could use an extra set of hands. In a few months we'll commence gathering for the trail drive down to the railroad pens." He paused, but they did not speak, so he said what he'd intended to tell them. "It's four days down an' four days back. We take a wagon . . . If you're feelin' up to it I'd be pleased to have you come along."

The girl said nothing but her colour mounted. Her brother, though, could not keep it back. "We can ride pretty good, Mister Thomas. We can herd cattle too."

Jawn Henry nodded about that, toyed with the idea of telling them not to drive other people's cattle but all he did say was: "It's not a good idea to drive cattle just to be drivin' them. That way they lose weight. There's plenty of work in the fall when we got to make the gather and the drive."

The girl reached to lightly touch Jawn Henry's hand. "Mister Thomas . . . "

He nodded without answering.

"Axel and me talked . . . If we could live here . . . "

Jawn Henry surprised himself. He leaned, kissed the girl's cheek and straightened back to say, "We'd be

real pleased to have you live with us
. . . By any chance you got kinfolk?"

"Back east," the girl replied. "Maw
had a sister back there. She's got six
children."

"Any other kin folks?"

"No. Paw didn't have any an' that
women back east is all maw had,
that she ever talked about." The
girl watched Jawn Henry's face. In
a smaller voice she also said, "We're
good workers, Mister Thomas. Axel's
real strong. Him an' me worked in the
potato patch. We helped paw roof the
soddy. We could work hard for you."

Jawn Henry arose from the bed
clearing his throat. He held out a
rough hand to the girl. She took it,
he squeezed and she squeezed back.
Axel stood up, someday he would be
as tall as Jawn Henry and most likely
a lot thicker.

He and Jawn Henry also shook
hands, but without any squeezings.
Axel had a bashful streak. He had a
little trouble, but he eventually said,

"Belinda an' me is real handy. We done a lot — "

Jawn Henry mussed the boy's hair. "All you got to do for a while is eat hearty an' mind your sister does the same."

He walked out into the gloomy hallway, hesitated to again clear his throat, then went to the kitchen where Bessie was making beef broth as Doctor Farrar had told her to do.

She turned from the stove, wiped her hands on her apron and looked steadily at her husband. "Are you catching a cold, Jawn Henry?"

"No, I'm not catching a cold. Whatever give you that idea?"

"Your eyes are watery."

Jawn Henry fished for a blue bandana, blew lustily and shook his head. Women!

Bessie went back to work at the stove. "It would be nice if they could stay with us, wouldn't it?"

"Yes."

"Can they stay, Jawn Henry?"

He scowled. "Well now why ask me something like that? Of course they can stay . . . They don't seem to have no kinfolk. Their paw didn't an' their maw has a sister back east somewhere who's already got six young ones."

Bessie turned, beaming. "They need us."

"They sure as hell need someone, Bessie."

"Jawn Henry . . . If you didn't swear in the house around them . . . "

He regarded his wife for a moment. There were going to have to be changes for a damned fact. He arose to go outside, and smiled at her. If he had to be a mite careful it wouldn't kill him, and it would be worth it to see his wife beam like she was doing now.

He was at the door before she said, "How is your back? Did it pain you the last few days?"

It hadn't, and right now that surprised him. "Feels fine, Bess. Feels like it used to."

She was pleased. "Doctor Farrar is

a good medicine man, isn't he?"

Jawn Henry opened the door, closed it behind himself and trudged in the direction of the barn. Changes yes, he'd make them, but nothing on gawd's earth was ever going to make him like that sour-faced stringbean who dressed like a damned undertaker!

## THE END